PENGUIN BOOKS

LOCKDOWN LOVERS

Michael O'Sullivan is a writer and academic based in Hong Kong. He has published 12 books on literature, philosophy and education. His most recent book Cloneliness was published by Bloomsbury in 2019. His poetry and essays appear in Times Higher Education, Voice and Verse, Asian Cha and PEN Hong's Kong's recent Hong Kong 20/20.

Lockdown Lovers

MICHAEL O'SULLIVAN

PENGUIN BOOKS

An imprint of Penguin Random House

PENGUIN BOOKS

USA | Canada | UK | Ireland | Australia
New Zealand | India | South Africa | China | Southeast Asia

Penguin Books is part of the Penguin Random House group of companies
whose addresses can be found at global.penguinrandomhouse.com

Published by Penguin Random House SEA Pte Ltd
9, Changi South Street 3, Level 08-01,
Singapore 486361

First published in Penguin Books by Penguin Random House SEA 2021

ISBN 9789814954129

Typeset in Adobe Caslon Pro by Manipal Technologies Limited, Manipal

www.penguin.sg

I

Hong Kong
February–March, 2020

John

The only place to write now is in this 24-hour McDonald's surrounded by disease and decay. No one bothers me here. I can sip on this free cup of warm water for as long as I wish. The only place to feel the stale odour of envy and failure slough off me like a skin. Here I am surrounded by the push of humanity in this city of death and disease. Already I have seen that familiar lurch in the street from a woman whose cough is so strong it knocks her off her stride. Already I have passed the hundreds of shivering locals in the long queue snaking around the block and up to Watsons on Fuk Man Street. They've been there for twelve hours in the cold all to pick up a fifty-dollar box of facemasks that no one is even sure will work. Already I've seen the tired expressions of the old men and women with the hoses from the sanitation trucks hosing down the dirt and filth of the streets. The spray from the streets splashes my bare calves as I pass and I wonder if the virus is already mutating inside me.

They have new words to manage this disease: walking incubators, walking carriers, hazmat suits, self-surveillance, self-quarantine. They've closed the borders, cancelled all flights. Anyone returning from abroad must stay indoors for fourteen days, self-isolating. If a student comes near me, I have to inform the authorities, get the student to fill in a health declaration form. Ask them to douse themselves in alcohol before leaving the building. All to avoid what the authorities now call in their emails 'physical interactions'. We must avoid each other at all costs. Close all post-offices, banks, markets, Apple stores, running tracks and public gyms. Outlaw the massage parlours, the foot-massage joints, the saunas and spas. I have already been requested to designate two of my closest colleagues to act as 'Disease Control' and 'Prevention' managers. Two colleagues with no medical training. Two colleagues who have worked in offices all their working lives. How can I let them do it? To put themselves in the frontlines like this. Simply because they are at the lowest rung of this academic corporation.

It's the waiting that does it. We wait for the numbers of casualties to increase. We listen to news reports and await texts from staff and senior management. Is your family okay? Stay healthy. Stay safe. At the back of our minds, we know that no one knows where this disease comes from or how one gets infected. We're simply waiting for the virus to peak. 'Peak' they say. Like a share option or a house price. And that's how they understand everything here. I have grown immune to their talk. It used to bother me. Now I take it on board, engage with it.

At least the government keeps itself in the news. When quizzed at a press conference about their slow response and lack of visible efforts during the crisis, the Chief Health Officer says, 'We can assure the public that we will keep the crematoriums running twenty-four hours a day.'

Kwok-ying

It's about dealing with the dead, not the living. The stark objective economic outlook of this city is already about dealing with diminishing returns. How to deal with those expendable elements? A certain culling is necessary, and we need to be honest and alert the public. You might not be dead yet, but death is coming down the tracks. How you prevent yourself from getting there is your own business, not ours. We in the Health Department will pick up the tab only when you've lost that particular battle. It's like what the *gweilo* (literally 'ghost-man' or white-skinned foreigner) said to me after typhoon Mangkhut, with the thousands of trees down, 'I guess it's nature's way of cleaning up.' Who knows . . . maybe this disease is the same. Maybe this is what the human race needs. Haven't we seen the end already in Marvel's Avengers? Didn't Thanos believe it was for the best too? To kill off half of humanity. And where better to start than in the world's most populous country. Start the culling here. Scientifically it makes sense. Scientifically I get it. But when you're a living, breathing entity in the midst of a global culling, it's a different proposition altogether.

Phoebe

So the rumour is that a Chinese scientist stole samples of deadly viruses from some lab in Canada and smuggled them into China. One local scientist says that part of the code of the new virus is identical to AIDS. Draw your own conclusions. Smuggled in, they were to be worked on in the new biolab in Wuhan. Some say it was in preparation for biological warfare. But get this—this new biolab is coincidentally in the same city as the local seafood market that is splashed on all the front pages and in all the news stories. Its dilapidated wrought iron gate closed shut at the front entrance of an old public market building, now deserted. We know the upshot. It went viral. Yes, blame the seafood, the clams and the mussels. Or better still, blame the other nameless 'wild animals' they sell there. 'Wild animals' they won't name with any certainty. The bats and the snakes, the rats and the civets. Blame the defenceless wild animals and not the men and women in hazmat suits putting live cultures of the world's most dangerous viruses into petri dishes while chatting about *Joker* or K-Pop. Don't blame the guys WeChatting and dreaming up chat-up lines as they transfer samples. And in another story, a disgruntled lab employee loses it. Maybe he's a jilted lover or a pure science nerd, someone who never has his nose out of his textbooks? Someone who experiences his first heartbreak between the aisles of live Ebola cultures. Someone who can't snap himself out of the funk he's in, his family and friends thousands of miles away in Xinjiang, perhaps in camps. Yes, a disgruntled lab worker, harbouring a vague sense of injustice about something the state did. He wraps a sample in a handkerchief and goes into the busiest place in town he can think of after work. The crowds milling around the seafood market. The big tanks of squirming sea life. Just drop it in. Drop the dish in. It'll open of its own accord. Drop it in.

Yes, blame the seafood market, the wild animals being sold there, and the locals—the poor locals who shop there because the supermarkets are too expensive. Big business is never to blame, or government with its biolab and its biological weapons programme. It's the sea urchins, the crayfish and the stingrays with their deadly tails. Those very same stingrays, idling now along the promenade of our fishing village. Waiting to be prised open for the pot. Yes, blame them and keep the crematoriums burning.

I remember the morning that we heard a local man had been infected. I'd only just been elected as a District councillor. Well, it seems he had visited Macau the week before. The doctors couldn't rule out that he had been infected locally. 'There could be a secret "carrier" in the city.' He was from a public housing estate in Tuen Mun. It triggered a desperate search for facemasks. Chemists were quickly sold out. There is an art to the purchase of facemasks. Stalk your branch of Watsons, queue at all hours, and don't be fooled by the two-ply merchants.

John

The photograph of the man in black, lying supine on a pavement in Wuhan, plastic bag in his left hand, his body lying neatly as if put in position for the coffin, shook us a little. He was found one block away from the main virus treatment hospital in Wuhan. Dressed in a black coat, black pants and black shoes with a face mask up to his eyes, it was as if he lay in state on the pavement, his eyes staring up at the sky, his grey hair showing at the sides. The news report said he was in his sixties. One expected a body that had just been struck down by this deadly coronavirus to be convulsed in agony. Shouldn't his limbs be contorted and twisted? Hadn't he writhed in the throes of death? Where were the signs of the resistance and the struggle? But, no, the body lay flat as if he had just decided to bed down for the day and had drifted off as he stared at the clouds above. His body didn't lie adjacent to the buildings, down an alleyway, or in some street corner. It was right in the centre of this busy, main street pavement. It was as if he had died as some kind of afterthought, as a by the way. Preoccupied with other matters, the body had, mid-stroll, given up and collapsed. Was suffering so common to these people that no pain was ever taken as a sign that the end was coming? Is this what it was like being a 'carrier'? Did death come so suddenly as to be unexpected? Was there no warning sign, no intimation of the approaching end? Nothing to make you want to move in closer to the wall so that your fall would not make you such a public spectacle?

Or, worse still, had he laid *himself* out neatly in the centre of the pavement knowing he would pass at any moment?

And where was he going? What was in the plastic bag? Was he going to admit himself into the hospital one block away? Or did he simply acknowledge that there was no point going there because all who left, invariably left for the mortuary? Had he decided to walk these streets until the end, safe in the knowledge that when he fell, at least his body would be close to a hospital where people in hazmat suits with canisters of disinfectant spray at the ready could come quickly to clean up the pavement? They disinfected the stretch of pavement he had lain on as soon as they zipped his body up and took it away. The photo showed two staff in hazmat suits standing close to his body. They were casting their eyes about like astronauts on some new undiscovered planet.

Was his last lunch preserved uneaten in the plastic bag by his side? Would they give it as much care as they gave the last lunch of that Tollund Man who was found preserved in the bogs of Denmark? What would the archaeologists learn from his soup noodles or dumplings? Had he concocted some kind of remedy that he had hoped would save him? Or was there a hastily-scribbled manifesto in the bag, advising all Wuhan residents to rise up in protest against the city authorities?

Phoebe

The vegetable shelves were empty again today. No sign of any of the green-leaf vegetables, *choi sum*, *pak choi*, Chinese kale. Bread and rice were gone too. People were hoarding and buying early. In the end, I gave up on the vegetables. It was a choice between cucumbers and thirty-three-dollar Brussels sprouts from the Netherlands. When I got outside on to the streets in Sai Kung Centre, I took the mask off. It was as radical as I could be these days. I walked to the pier. I'd been reading earlier about the different grades of facemask. Reading on my phone that is. It was becoming how I read more and more these days. It seems the virus can be spread by big droplets and by micro-droplets. I'd read how a flu virus can hang around in the air in a room six hours after the carriers have left. No gaps must be showing between facemask and face. It was impossible. What about those *gweilos* with the big noses? The big-boned Europeans? They'd have to sellotape the edges of the mask to their faces. They were sitting ducks. The newspaper articles said that the common or garden variety facemask offers only six times more protection. The really fancy ones can offer a hundred times more protection. But six times more than what? Six times more than nothing? In a street where tiny micro-droplets might be hanging in the air at each and every step does a hundred times more than nothing mean anything at all?

John

I sat down at a bench near the pier and stared out at the junks and old fishing boats, at the luxury yachts and golf island catamarans all bobbing on the water. Would living out there keep you safe? Surely this sea breeze could blow away any lingering micro-droplets? If I only could rent a boat and live out there. Far from shore but not too far. Take a month's provisions. Ten five-litre bottles of water, fifty tins of tuna and miso, pot noodles, chocolate. Some carrots to munch on. Bananas. Maybe I'd be safer. Finish off this monologue. Write to ward off the boredom. Imagine the perspective I'd have from out there. Looking back the whole time at the shore. Hearing the cries of the land-dwellers as the yellow mist engulfed them. Waiting for the crowds to dissipate, to approach dry land. See the piers and boardwalks fill up and know it was safe to go back in out of the water.

Today they told us no foreigner who has been in China in recent weeks can get into the US. My wife is ethnically Chinese. She has no overseas passport. Our son was born here. It's only the beginning. Soon there will be more restrictions, more barriers. We can't leave now. We're staying put. I was talking to a local bread-seller about it today. I could tell she was eager to talk once I got started:

- 'Crazy times, aren't they?'
- 'Did you hear? No Chinese allowed into the US?'
- 'Yes, I heard. It's . . .'
- 'The US, the country that everyone believes is the best for human rights is the first to give up on human rights.'

- 'Yes, I see. I hadn't thought of it that way . . .'
- 'Yes, but so many people in Hong Kong think this, that the US is the home of human rights.'

I took my change from her. She'd obviously been thinking long and hard about it. She wanted to change the focus, to turn the talk away from the local restrictions.

- 'Not many Hong Kong people know this.'

I didn't follow her now, but I could sense her passion and I felt I should play along.

- 'Yes, it's true. Yes, I know what you mean. Human rights are one of the first things that go out of the window.'

I try to remind myself that people have different perspectives on the whole thing. We don't all follow the same headlines. We managed to say this much before we realized our facemasks weren't on. With the facemasks on, talk became a little self-conscious and eventually petered out.

- 'But aren't you a little bit scared?'
- 'No, people aren't scared. It's the government that makes us scared.'

Kwok-ying

Now there is an outbreak of bird flu in a chicken farm in Hubei province just south of the epicentre of the epidemic. 450 chickens in a farm of about 600 were found dead. They culled about 800 chickens in the area. No animal to human transmission has been reported. What would it take for it to jump to humans? What kind of mutation? And how would that mutation happen? If you took up living 24x7 with the diseased chickens in their coop would that be enough? Ingesting vast quantities of the diseased chickens?

I took a day off today. Drove out to Sai Kung. At Sai Kung Bakery people are queuing for the famous bolobaos. At least it's not for masks. Takes me back to my childhood in Shatin. We used to drive out to Sai Kung for the bolobao. Soft, fresh, white bread buns coated with a thick crust of golden pineapple sugar. They queue out the door and along the streets. Twelve dollars a bun. All wearing facemasks. But, as soon as they get those bolobaos, the masks come off. Their mouths launch into the soft, loamy bread and the crusts of sugar as if they were the last buns on earth. You can forget about your micro-droplets, I've got my bolobao. It's the most famous bakery in New Territories. Sparrows creep to the door of the bakery pecking at the crumbs that have fallen from the hot trays going back and forth between the ovens and the shelves in the shop. The sweet, tangy smell of burnt pineapple sugar and freshly-baked bread fills the air. I inhale deeply. Something in this is not about disease. The way we relish the warm buns, tearing into them and the soft white flesh of their interiors. A moment to forget all our cares. Some kind of unconscious cleansing ritual. Biting into the piping hot buns in the wintry cold of the decades-old, dilapidated bakery in Sai Kung almost makes us feel protected. The fresh, hot buns and the white ceramic cups and saucers of homebrewed coffee leave the seafood markets of Wuhan far behind. We are on the final day of the extended Chinese New Year holiday and we try to forget that it is only because of the disease that the holiday is so long. We inhale deeply the aroma of freshly-baked bolobao and sip our homebrewed coffee, little puddles forming in the white saucers of our brimming cups.

The Party is changing its narrative we were informed. Shi makes an admission. He knew about the virus on 09 January. Made oral demands about it to Politburo members. He appeared next in public on 23 January. Made his Party speech on 20 January, but did not mention the virus. Big problem. Why didn't he mention it? The new narrative is one of heroes and villains. Paint Dr Lu Weiming as a hero. But release his personal emails to colleagues saying he 'would do what the Party ordered'. He felt the Party would ultimately 'get us through this'. Yes, he is a hero, but a hero following the Party line. Get this out.

John

The dogs waiting for their owners by the 7-Eleven have rich coats and lazy gaits. They know how to get through an epidemic. Their muzzles prevent them from barking. Our facemasks don't stop us talking. We stare out at unrecognizable faces and ask ourselves, 'Do I seem more assertive behind a face mask?' 'Is there anything they do not see behind the mask?' Our eyes are doing so much of the talking for us now. Nothing else is visible. But then the eyes are sometimes the part we wish to avoid. Is it helping us look each other in the eye? I'm not so sure.

Down by the pier, a shoal of fish congregates by the overflow gulley from the drains that lead back to the fish restaurants. Globules of oil explode into colour as they float past beneath me in the seawater. In the mix of dirty water, I see bits of old shell, leftover fish parts, shreds of fish skin. All being lapped up by the fish leaping out of the water in exuberance. The perennial life of this seaside town still shows no signs of being bowed down by the virus. Dogs still bark, fish still scavenge, and the old, brown kites still circle in the skies above.

But disease is always there in the background. It's the yardstick with which we measure all life now. It's the constant presence we live to dodge. In pre-disease times there was no sense of such an awareness of mortality. We let it slip. Now, we know that the dividing walls between us and death are at least felt. They have moved from out beyond silence to hearsay and gossip.

A Jehovah Witness comes up to me with a booklet. I talk to her about the blood transfusion argument. She is ready for it.

\-   'I am a nurse and there are other ways to save the body at such times.'

What can I say? She talks about the beauty of nature in Sai Kung and I take the booklet from her. I say to myself that I will read it out of respect, but I eventually throw it away.

\-   'How many congregation members do you have in Sai Kung?'
\-   'About seven thousand.'

I try to picture what their church might look like. A cramped set of rooms above a gym or supermarket. Seven thousand people worshipping; the devoted crying out together.

Phoebe

The video of the hospital in Wuhan went viral. Comments on Vimeo said there were at least eight bodies shown. I saw a van full of zipped-up bodies. There were bodies on trolleys and in waiting rooms and one could not be sure whether they were dead or alive. But it went viral and the caption said that the guy who had filmed it had been arrested. He gave us this before he was locked away. Possibly shot. Another viral video of Wuhan showed three men in white coats, light blue operating theatre gowns and facemasks striding down a narrow road into a housing estate with rifles slung over their shoulders and revolvers pointing forwards. But this reporter got it uploaded before he was downloaded. He got some of the truth out. Others say he was put in forced quarantine.

So many conspiracy theories now. Some say there is no virus. It has all been staged to knock the edge off the USA's demands for a trade war. To get some leverage.

John

The only place left for me to sit and write about this is here in the 24-hour McDonald's in Sai Kung. With people still milling around, I can let the general hubbub take my mind off the call of daily duties for a few moments. I can sip for free on some warm water and they never hurry me out. They never ask me to leave. I'm away from Sam, our sick boy. He wakes me every morning at about 4 or 5. I feed him milk, rub his back, change his nappy and try to stop his cough. I try to get the mucus up from the back of his throat. But it's no good. And then I rock him. I rock him as I pace for kilometres on the tiles of my flat. Pacing the tiles, trying to keep my anger out of my body. My frustration at these hours given up. I never was very patient and this rocking and pacing tests my patience like nothing has done before. The muscles ache in my arms and lower back, but still he won't sleep. No, it annihilates patience and fills the void with passive routine. I do the mornings and Sue does the nights. It is not Wordsworth's wise passiveness I often feel at such times.

In McDonald's, all the women behind the counter wear facemasks up to their eyes. All the customers wear facemasks too. We become faceless. Staring eyes. At the doctor's yesterday, as she spoke about my boy, I couldn't hold her stare. I mean there is nothing else to stare at but the eyes. Only the eyes. It's the blank of the facemask and then those staring, fearful eyes on everyone. We have become ciphers, placeholders for emptiness. We have given our identity away to the disease. For sure, it has already taken our identities, already killed us off insofar as we are capable of being known by others. We walk around aimlessly without faces. All public facilities are closed, all community halls, all sportsgrounds, all major bank branches. All flights out of Hong Kong are suspended. The malls stay open, but the shelves are empty. No bleach, no toilet rolls, no handwash, no sanitary towels, no rice, no alcohol wipes, no Dettol. The list grows every day. Soon we won't function as we ought. A viral photo showed a middle-aged man with a trolley full of sanitary towels. We walk the streets aimless and faceless. It's a vision of a dystopian future realized. When either pollution, or drug resistance, or disease become everyday dangers. Our individuality lost forever. Our fearful, darting eyes indistinguishable. Our heads shaved and scarved to prevent infestation or infection. And can we even be sure that the eyes will remain? Many people are recommending dark glasses to protect the eyes from the micro-droplets. Soon there will be nothing to see, nothing to encounter. My own colleagues now wear dark glasses all the time. They've become unrecognizable. We walk aimlessly in the diseased streets meeting no one, not knowing anyone. Food and supplies hoarded at home, we only come out to walk in the open spaces that are left to us. Even the public toilets are empty.

So, I write to remind myself of my individuality. To remind myself of the person I once was. For in this unrecognizable, anonymous world I realize that I am a person not only because of how I see myself but also because of how others see me. No one sees me now, so I no longer know who I am. Even my ailing wife wears a facemask at home. Sometimes I weep on the sofa when she has gone to bed remembering the softness of her lips. To think that our lips once touched in passion. To think they then only touched in fear. To think they now never touch at all. And how we used to hold hands. At the most mundane moments. On the bus. Taking Sam out for lunch. Our only son. Our precious bundle of joy. Now, the smell of alcohol disinfectant is like the smell of life itself and it screams out at me 'Don't Touch!' It feels like she has left me already. It's like Sam is her whole world now. Since I am a danger to Sam, I am a threat, I am unwanted.

Writing it out helps me. It helps me remember not only the images but the sensations as well, and the sensations are all that now remind us of our humanity. People ask why the violence started, why doctors had their facemasks ripped off by patients and angry relatives, why sick patients self-checked out and roamed the streets and the markets and the public transport networks with abandon. People said that they were like animals. But no one revealed their faces when they spoke to the cameras. Not only for fear of getting infected. Every cough is frightening they said. The government never loosened its iron grip despite all the suffering and death. People ask why they started raiding hospital storerooms and the chemists and hoarding the medicines in a bunker guarded by the army. The thousands crawling to the gates. If only they knew that the stockpiles didn't offer any protection.

Now the new normal is hiding oneself away in public. Five of us might sit shoulder to shoulder at the window seats at McDonald's, but we are faceless and silent. When we eat and drink our faces emerge from the masks. But only so we can fill our faces with food. Our ravenous eyes stare out at the grey street and the parked cars. Or we watch games on our phones, staring out at the rain, mentally attacking anyone we see without a mask.

I remember, with something like fondness now, when the first death was announced in our district. Neighbouring cities had been devastated and we had closed nearly all border entries. We congratulated ourselves on our good health. Our good health! Can you believe it? Reduced to walking facemasks with cavernous, darting eyes and we called it 'good health'. The port and the ferry terminal remained open. The Sea Bridge from Zhuhai had been mobbed by protesters stopping buses from entering the city. The first death was a thirty-nine-year-old man with 'underlying conditions'. It was a new euphemism for dying from the virus. The next three infected cases were all locals who had never crossed the borders in recent weeks. They had no underlying conditions worth mentioning. Poverty could never be mentioned. Malnutrition could not be mentioned. Despair could not even be credited. They now spoke of 'silent carriers' in the city. It seemed redundant. Who was going to shout from the rafters 'I'm infected'? They spoke of an outbreak being expected in the city. Of the virus not peaking for weeks. The epidemiologist from the top university had been waiting twenty years for this. SARS had made the careers of all his seniors. No matter how much he published, no matter how many patents he was awarded, he could never match what they had done. They were local heroes. Images of them in facemasks standing over the beds of SARS victims in the Prince of Wales Hospital haunted everyone's dreams. He could do it this time. He could put his body on the line.

Phoebe

The virus was not just a disease, it was a way of life, a way of being. Virus funds and virus plays in the stock market and in sports sprang up all over the net. In casinos and sportsgrounds players modelled the power of the virus. The speed of attack, the incubation period, the silent carriers, the manner of relating to others all became metaphors taken from virus history. To pass on something was never the same again. Sharing was corrupted. Giving took on a dangerous hue. To give became associated only with disease. All the rest was only offering.

The photo today in the *South China* from the HouShenShan (Fire God Mountain) New Hospital in Wuhan shows a long line of closely-packed beds, maybe twenty, with barely any walking space between them. The head of each bed rests against the foot of the adjoining bed with no spaces in between. All the face-masked patients lying in, or sitting in, or standing on, the beds are young men. The young man closest to the camera is lying flat, the blanket drawn up to his waist, a large hardback textbook open on his chest. It looks like a law book or a medicine textbook. Surrounded by disease, he still has his dream. He's turning away from the other men in the other beds. Despite his illness, he's preparing for the law course that has been delayed because of the virus he now carries inside.

Panic-buying began this week. With the border closed, rumours spread of food shortages. The government did its utmost to stave off people's fears. 'We have thirteen million tonnes of rice in storage.' Long lines of shoppers waited for new shipments of toilet paper and tissues. A man in his fifties was snapped on Instagram with a trolley full of sanitary towels. The check-out woman asked me for my 'Octopus' card for payment and for a minute all I could think of was the seafood market in Wuhan.

John

Simply writing anything sparks a new train of thought. I write to find a way out of myself. The virus unifies us. At home we have more hours together. I have become more of a stay-at-home dad for Sue and our son, Sam. My sick boy seems to improve. He never goes out. When I come home this, small human being cries at the top of his voice for me to take him up in his arms. It would melt a heart of ice. What is the saying again? I have fears that in reading less I am less versatile. So be it. They want us to publish and publish but in the end our words only ever skirt the surface of things. So long as I can still communicate something. That's what matters. One million words later, I must still communicate but in a way that speaks. I look at the twelve hardback books we've published that gather dust on my shelf. They are like old photos. Old MRI scans of my brain—of which I actually have three sets never opened. The books are like this. Some kind of imaging. Maybe even a therapeutic marker. My war with words. Two million words later. Two million printed words later and I still can't communicate. These academic books on my shelf. Pillars to blockage.

Meanwhile, I only write now in the 24-hour McDonald's where the cup of warm water that I sip is free. My writing and everything about this performance here today is free. I have no contractual obligations to write this. My employee contract will be done as soon as this goes live. The old form of writing has almost been forgotten. The virus has helped me find a new way to communicate. The woman next to me finishes her coffee and replaces her mask. We are becoming comfortable with our anonymity. We only blossom and reveal ourselves when we mask up or when we take the mask off for the Zoom screen during class. Soon we will dread the acknowledgement of the face. All that flesh. All that individuality.

Phoebe

Today the doctor who blew the whistle—that's how they keep describing it here—passed away. Dr Lu wrote to his colleagues and friends about a 'SARS-like virus' and he was arrested for rumour-mongering. He and eight others. So far 670 million people have viewed the hashtag 'Dr Lu passed away'. People wrote gigantic messages of sympathy in Chinese characters in the snow. Professors and those in the know claim it could be a seismic event like the death of Premier Hu Xiyuan in 1989 before the Square Incident. But they advise that the response cannot be too heavy-handed as the authorities risk undermining the already low morale of those trying to control the virus. Eighty-one have died today and there are 34,000 in hospitals if numbers are to be believed. I think of their families as I sit here in McDonald's. None of them asked to die. They leave tears and mourning behind. I offer up a secular prayer for them.

John

Panic buying continues here. The quest to protect one's own remains a top priority for the faceless and the anonymous. Queues of anonymous buyers, each one dragging two twelve-packs of toilet roll behind them, congratulate themselves on being ahead of the game. I met Joseph, an old friend, who is going back to the US. He was leaving at the end of the month. He had an argument about everything.

- 'So what's your take on the whole thing, Joseph?'
- 'On this madness? On all this? Well, don't get me started. You know I'll never stop. I've long thought Hong Kong has an infection mentality. *You* know that. Not only a siege mentality but an infection mentality. Fear of change and fear of invasion from the north found its perfect metaphor in SARS. SARS too came from the North yunno, from the mainland.'
- 'Ah yes, but surely that's going a bit far, isn't it?'
- 'I'm not so sure. "Doesn't it prove our theories?" the anonymous faces I see around shout out to me. How much can we give up to this infection mentality? Closing ourselves off. Closing the borders. Closing the schools, the banks, the sportsgrounds. Closing in on our masked selves. Staying indoors. Staying as close to the familiar and the disinfected as possible. I can see people getting an almost silent sense of liberation from this retreat into self-isolation.'
- 'But the two aren't connected at all really. The reaction to this virus and then the protests. Surely, the protests started off

with those skirmishes with the parallel traders coming from the mainland . . .'

- 'Yes, but mainland shoppers disappeared a long time ago. The parallel traders too. Now they can say "Finally we have Hong Kong for Hong Kongers." Sinn Féin. Ourselves alone. Isn't that what our Irish relatives would have called it? What the protests began, the virus has finished.'
- 'C'mon now, Joseph, that's pushing it . . .'
- 'No, I still say it's an infection mentality. Hong Kongers reclaim their city through an infection mentality. You can see the arcades reclaimed by locals. Universities are closed too and they're asking all the returning mainlanders to self-quarantine for fourteen days. They will never feel welcome again. The Dream of Localism is realized in all but name. The retreat behind the mask unleashes the dream of reclaiming the city. Hong Kong finds its identity the more isolated it becomes. The more its people retreat into anonymity.'

I listened and smiled.

- 'Joseph, you won't miss this place, so I'm guessing?'
- 'Of course, I will. Where else could I be so opinionated without fearing backlash?'
- 'Well, that's it, you see. It won't always be so easy to say what you want . . .'
- 'Without this sense of being an outsider, I'd never be so sure of myself. I speak of the isolation of Hong Kongers but you know there's a big white elephant in the room here! You know this better than anyone. [He smiled] No one is more isolated in this city than the *gweilo*! And you're only likely to get ever more isolated. You know it, John. They'll be coming for you soon. So, take it all with a pinch of salt. I still think I'm on to something.'

We smiled and drank from our coffees. We had our facemasks hanging down past our chins. He smiled and drained the last of his decaf coffee. Our receding hairlines, eye problems, and leg cramps were our next topics of conversation. They reminded us our bodies had seen better days. And our minds too. Now we were changing countries again. Him going back to San Francisco and me still in Hong Kong but aiming for Ireland when this was all over. Hong Kong had been the only place we'd managed to spend quality time together since the Camino to Santiago de Compostela. We'd bonded over the seven long weeks it took us to walk across Spain back in the summer of '96 or '97. Almost a quarter of a century and we still felt we were talking like young men. The curse of the middle-aged man. He never knows how to shut down the twenty-something inside him. And when I say we bonded on the Camino, I mean we had learned we could come together by finding out how far we could go with our complaints to each other. When we got to Leon, about half way through the Camino, we knew we had to do it alone. There was only so much we could take, but admitting to each other that we needed space told us a lot about how close we were. We were comfortable letting off steam with each other and then disappearing from each other's lives, no questions asked, sometimes for years on end. But when we met up again, we picked up where we had left off. Any city, any group of people, could be a means for further self-discovery. Joseph had been to most places. I'd only lived in five countries so far. But it gave us enough to work off of.

When we finished our coffees, we went our separate ways. He was flying out the next day. We parted not knowing when or where we would meet again. And yet it felt like the most natural thing in the world. I walked back to my flat. Our sick boy was crying. I could hear him when I entered the village. Three storeys up, his cries were the cries of my boy. Something of my voice in them. The domestic helper from flat two was mopping the steps

with bleach. She clutched the mop closely and backed herself into
the corner of the stairwell to let me pass. It was what I was used to.
I said, '*jo san*,' and she returned my greeting, but the awkward look
on her face as she made herself as small as she could in the corner
of the stairwell was one of fear and distrust. We were capable of a
whole new level of infection, us *gweilo*s. Bleach and Dettol were
no match for what we brought to this city and to its people.

I missed Joseph when he left, but I didn't dwell on it. Since his
divorce he seemed a little more reckless. He'd given up the booze
and now resorted to herbs to relax. I recall him visiting one year
and telling me about an experience he had after taking a new herb.
He was sitting back in a chair in the pizzeria. His face looked like
he was reliving a nightmare.

-    'Imagine if all the voices—you know the voices you hear in
     your head sometimes—were all shouting and all at the same
     time. It was like that. Or imagine the DVD sound where it
     is stuck and you have this repetitive DVD whine going on
     and on, a kind of metallic repetitive DVD whine. Or do you
     remember *Inception*—yunno the movie—imagine if all the
     different dimensions—how many do we have?—were folding
     in on themselves but that you were part of the destruction, you
     were a part of their destruction. And not only this, but you feel
     like you are nothing but a mind. You look down on your own
     body and all you see are these lines, these grid lines, as if you're
     coming back together. And you look at a bottle or an object
     and you see the different dimensions all coming together
     around the bottle. All the different dimensions that go in to
     make up the bottle, you see them consolidate simultaneously.'

Kwok-ying

Big crackdown on Chinese medicine. And about time too. They were getting away with murder. Pangolins and civets. Whatever next? Bat meat? Dragon balls? Chinese medicines were as bad as that goop shit on Netflix. Psychedelic cures, my arse! I've seen more honesty in a Politburo meeting.

The remedies are useless here, and they're useless everywhere. Once, I saw a lamb placenta facial product in Mannings. Herbal remedies were always no better than alchemy unless you said you were taking it as part of a Chinese medicine course of treatment. That was sacred here, but wasn't that where it all started? The pangolin, the only scaled mammal left to stew. He may have been the missing link in helping the virus shift from fruit bats to humans. 13.1 tons of pangolin scales were found in a container in Shenzhen in 2016. We reported it. Chinese wedding banquets are also known to include a course featuring the odd pangolin foetus soup said one local whom I interviewed. Pangolin scales are prescribed to treat arthritis, menstrual cramps and to help lactating women. But, today's report must be on how the poaching became too aggressive. Make 'Scaling Back Pangolin-scale Sales' your subject heading. Thousands of pangolins were harvested and dumped in silos in a wasteland in Shenzhen before they were stripped of the scales. We reported it. With photos too. Stripping them of their scales is dirty business. The scales must be dry and clean of all flesh to be sold. You can imagine the pain for the pangolin. Each pangolin can have thousands of scales. Being stripped of the scales while alive is surely extreme torture. Torturing thousands of pangolins takes time. We didn't include this in the report to Head Office. Sometimes the pangolins would be left half-dead in sheds and tents. This was not covered in our report. Bats would come and feed. The bats may well ingest the infected bodies of the pangolins that we reported on. However, this year, the pangolins in the Wuhan seafood and animal market were unhealthy looking. They were shedding their scales and their long snouts seemed to be oozing a kind of mucus. Some research papers that we are trying to suppress suggest that the bats which had fed on this creature—the pangolin—had become infected. We are working on the disappearance of pangolins from markets everywhere and on the disappearance of those papers. How could parents with young kids ever visit our markets with so many pangolins about? We will lead with a story.

I only got into this health lark because I dropped out of medicine. In the end, the long hours with textbooks and no money got to me. I only signed up in the first place for the salary and the crisp white coat. My mother was distraught when I broke it to her. But now, I'm basically telling doctors what to do, who to admit, and where to put them.

Pangolin

The culprit has been found they tell us. The simple pangolin had no idea what it was starting. With thousands of its brothers and sisters being slaughtered, mutilated, and tortured every day in this corner of the Southern Hubei forests, it found itself distressed. It didn't have the same appetite, one might say. It was turned right off its food having to wade through the bloodied scales and entrails of its brothers and sisters every morning. Truth be told, it had relied on its brothers and sisters a little too much to catch and hoard most of the food stock. It was a somewhat lazy pangolin, but it knew it wasn't so unusual among its kind. But times were tough, and winter was approaching. Without sustenance it would not make it through the long, cold sleeps of winter. So, it went a little astray in its foraging. It felt delirious with hunger as the days grew shorter and closed about it earlier. It cried all night for its brothers and sisters but all it heard in response was the cackling and hawking of this new species camped by its favourite foraging spot. All it smelled was the whiff of burning smoke coughed up out of the mouths of the campers along with the reek of the charred remains of its own kind. It felt nauseous. It could feel something was not quite right. The creatures made strange noises and the way they ate made him sick to the stomach. This was a discovery. These were the animals who had taken his brothers and sisters. He was sure of it. He had heard talk in the wild of the multicoloured bipeds who lived out beyond the banyan and the evergreen lowlands. They were sometimes gods, sometimes beasts. He knew he must move away from his home, from the lands in which he had foraged since young. He must hunt near the rapids and the high lands. It was dead of night when he decided to set out. The night whispered to him as he foraged along the unfamiliar path. He saw black forms flying about overhead. A paw swiped instinctively, and he knew he had hit out at something. There was something squirming in the undergrowth just beyond his snout. He reached out, and before he really knew it, in making his final thrust, he found himself feasting. Was it a dream or a waking vision? He never could have claimed with any certainty, had he been questioned later, whether it had been the droppings or the entrails of the fruit bat that he had been feasting on. Whatever it was, he made it to morning and when he awoke, he had the remains before him at daybreak, for all to see. But before he could determine the nature of this miracle, of this manna from the heavens, two claws seemed to ensnare him and he was being lifted into the air. It was a kneejerk reaction to preserve his life. He lashed out with his claw and he knew he had sliced through something. He was dropped and was back in the undergrowth again. He heard something like a groan then a cough from what sounded like the new species he had seen on his foraging grounds the night before. He scurried with all his newfound energy, driving deeper and deeper into the thick undergrowth, not even noting if the sounds from his attacker were receding. He was now almost burrowing into the soil beneath the dense undergrowth. In the end he was convinced it was his decision to stop dead in the dense undergrowth that saved him as he heard the hoof beats of the multicoloured bipeds passing close by and then moving on.

John

My father tells me he is taking each day as it comes. I try to work this way. It took us a while, but in the end, I carved out a kind of routine. Otherwise, one is likely to slide into a dangerous state of apathy. Our sick boy's wailing wakes me between four and five in the morning. As I come to from out of my slumber and the already cloudy dreams of the night before, I see his small outline in the dark as he wails and clings to the arms of the cot. I roll out of the bed and take him in my arms. There is always the sense of this being something I was meant to do. How he fits snugly into my arms and down along my chest and then how his wailing stops as soon as I pick him up. I pat his back and try to get the mucus moving. The cough still comes from deep inside. My sick wife moves in the bed. I try not to wake her. I take him into the living room. I prepare the milk with the lights off and with him in one arm. It strains all my strength to mix the formula while he resists in my other arm. But it is the way I do it. I like the feeling of getting one over, of straining to multitask like this. I tell myself I am winning back a bit of time or effort. Who am I fooling? I sit on the sofa and he snuggles into me as I feed him. His mouth looks for the nipple and he is off again, silent and feeding. I have a few moments to gather myself. When he is fed, I take him up again and on a good morning he will be asleep in half an hour. I pace the long kilometres over the apartment tiles as I rock him. Sometimes I have to rest him against the back of a chair or support my legs with the sofa when the pain in my lower back comes on. When he is sound asleep, I lower him carefully into the cot, tug out the blanket from under him and place it gently over him again.

I bag all the rubbish in the kitchen and tie it up. I bag the rubbish in the bathroom and tie it up as well. I bag my son's soiled nappies. I take them out to the bins at the end of the village. When I get back, I wipe every surface with the alcohol wipes. I brush the floors and then mop them with floor cleaner and water. I mop the stairwell. I wash and steam the baby's bottles, nipples, spoons, bowls, syringes and dummies. I stack them in the plastic container I bought from Japan Home Centre. I then hear him crying again. I pick him up and the cycle continues. I change his nappy and see if he will take the leftover milk in the bottle. When my wife gets up, I shower. I wash my hands in alcohol wash. My wife and I clean the Combi high chair with disinfectant. We clean the pram and I strap him in. We attach the plastic cover for the pram so our boy is sealed in and protected from anyone who might want to touch him. We put on our surgical gloves and open two new surgical masks. My wife wears dark glasses now. I wouldn't recognize her if I didn't know it was she standing beside me. We are ready to take our walk in this the quietest time of the day.

My wife was dreaming of schooling him abroad. We had the plans *and* the passport. We only needed to do all the paperwork to leave. I had no job abroad, so I delayed. In the end, the paperwork seemed like too much work. So, we delayed. Now we are trapped here with all flights cut.

There is a woman called Selina in Sai Kung. She's an elderly woman who goes around talking to herself and giving impromptu lectures to people in McDonald's and Starbucks. Sometimes she comes right up to your table and raps the table with her fan.

-    'I am Princess Selina. I am a millionaire's heiress. I am Princess Selina.'

Today she was dressed in a short waist-length fur coat, a flowing white lace gown, three wide brimmed feather hats, black lace gloves, three facemasks and two flashy gold holdalls, the kind of holdall a designer label shop might give you for free if you shopped there enough.

-     'I am Princess Selina' she says. 'Ngoi hai Princess Selina.'

She walks around the half-empty McDonald's depositing her large gold holdalls willy-nilly across the tables. A group of Filipino women, their facemasks down, consider asking her if the seats around the tables with her holdalls are free. I can see the intent on their faces, but Selina is still talking to another group of customers she doesn't know. The Filipino women move away and sit outside.

-     'Princess Selina is here. The millionaire's heiress. Disinfect those tables. Where is my coffee? Don't you know I am Princess Selina?'

She seems to be ordering the staff around, but they only laugh among themselves when they think she can't see them. Behind her three facemasks and under her three wide-brimmed feathered hats, I notice her pale complexion and how her grey hair is dyed a light reddish brown. It makes her skin look paler. Her hands look old. She must be in her seventies. In this diseased city of anonymous faceless isolates, to hear her shouting aloud her identity is refreshing. All of a sudden, she reminds me of a character from a story I've been teaching. Gustav von Aschenbach meets an old man on the ferry as he arrives in a diseased Venice in Thomas Mann's *Death in Venice*. His leering eyes, old lip-sticked mouth, and rouged cheeks mock the slightly younger Aschenbach who is on a mission to rejuvenate himself in this border city at the very edge of old Europe. Mann, himself, had gone to Venice in 1911 as a younger man with his wife and brother. Away from Munich and family life, he was looking for artistic inspiration and he became preoccupied by a ten-year-old boy staying at the same hotel. Venice. Another border city on the edge of empire. A city on the borderlands between East and West. A few miles from Trieste whose borders once marked the edges of the Ottoman Empire. Border cities at the crossroads of great cultures where rules seem transitory and identity shifts quickly from fluid to sacred. Hong Kong, Venice, San Diego. Cities sought

out by those who like to have old certainties challenged. Mann's
most famous story would help launch his international career. It
was a career that took him to the United States where, in the '50s,
he spoke out against another 'State of Emergency', one sprung by
McCarthyism. 'Spiritual intolerance, political inquisitions, and
declining legal security, and all this in the name of an alleged "state
of emergency" . . . That is how it started in Germany.'

So many of the old Europeans came here too. Sunset cowboys
they called them. I always wondered how my coming out here
was seen by friends back home. FILTH some locals called them.
Failed in London Try Hong Kong. Was there any truth in it?
Border towns. Showy and edgy. Places where you might dodge
the bullet. Work an angle you couldn't work at home. All of
a sudden, I saw Princess Selina in a new light. Princess Selina
was an icon of the city. She was the city. I saw it clearly. A little
puffed up on former glories but now frayed around the edges
and unable to accept the new reality. Always wanting to remind
close neighbours of her special status. Pearl of the Orient. A
Special Administrative Region. But now the disease makes people
afraid. The special status is hard to sustain. We all walk about
with our faces masked, but lip-sticked and rouged underneath.
We are waging a war against reality. But the external grandeur's
fading. The old temples to commerce are boarded up and strewn
with graffiti. First, because of the protests and now, the virus.
We retreat to the only place left to retain our special opinion of
ourselves, our distinction, our fading grandeur. We retreat to the
gaudy memories of the past embodied by our own stories. The
isolating strengthens the fantasy. 'I'm a Millionaire's Heiress!' We
will listen to no one. They all don't get it. They all have it in for us.
This virus that has us isolating ourselves at all costs only confirms
our special status and the difficult task of infecting us. No one can
withstand infection like us. No one will be harder to infect than us.

Phoebe

They say the virus can survive for thirty-six hours on stainless steel. We are afraid to go out, to touch surfaces, to inhale the air. It's is a new experience for us. A friend tells me she thinks it's all manufactured, that there is no virus, and I lose it. My passion surprises me. I tell her we can't risk it. No one will get infected on our watch even if it is all a hoax. I can understand her saying it. Everyone feeds their own anger. I think about what she says as I pass an old-people's home off Man Nin Street. The doors are open to the street. I see buckets at the end of old unmade beds. An old man sits alone in unkempt pyjamas. It's for them we are doing this. I need to remind myself. Between the anti-vaxxers, the anti-westerners, and the anti-communists, I need a foothold sometimes. I need to remember that old man. The virus can give me that much focus.

The weather today is warm and humid. A low-lying fog hangs over Ma On Shan mountain. I read in the paper that they think it can now be spread by aerosol transmission. Tiny droplets, suspended in the air, swarming around. I walk the pier and imagine the bugs dyed blue in the air. An army of droplets. I read about the billions of locusts attacking crops in Sudan and Ethiopia. A plague of locusts on your house. The schoolgirl fear before the dreams and prophecies of Joseph in the Bible. Again and again he was asked to read the dreams of the Pharaoh to find a way to put off the plagues attacking the city. Today there are no dreams. Only the plagues.

I've been making homemade facemasks out of badminton shuttlecocks and home-cleansing remedies out of a range of chemicals. Left one bottle in the entrance of my building with a tag on its ingredients but no one touched it in thirty-six hours.

John

This morning I drink my coffee in a dilapidated coffee shop and bakery. An old woman at the next table squints at me. I see her staring intently whenever I look up. It's as if she's trying to understand how someone, a *gweilo* here, could look like me. My bright green windcheater above my running shorts. My bare, white, hairy legs. No socks. Only the black leather shoes. She has a slight smile as she squints my way. Then she says something to the middle-aged Chinese man with the tanned skin across the table from her. He smiles back but never looks my way. I feel his smile is about me. This lack of contact with each other feeds our paranoia. I keep in mind the suffering of the cities where hundreds are dying. Only a few hundred kilometres away. I need something real to focus on. Then, in the corner of my eye, something is moving. A giant cockroach appears out of a drain and I realize the legs of my stool are on one of the vents for the septic tank. I trace the movements of the cockroach across the concrete flags and see it dodge the steps of passers-by unaware of its presence. The danger we face is a bit like this. Never knowing when the virus will step on us.

These are the moments when we have time to ourselves. Even in lockdown we can't seem to find the time. An American comes into the shop and is greeted with a big hello. I can't command such a response. In all my years here. It's all I can do not to feel uncomfortable buying my *seung bun* and *yi gafe*, my scone and hot coffee. I try to find the cockroach again, but he's gone.

I came to Asia to follow a career dream. A dream I couldn't fulfil in the West. In the end, I also started a family. Destined to be frustrated where I grew up, I made for Asia and a contract of employment. It promised a livelihood where I could follow a path I felt I needed to explore. In those days, the need for a new form of expression may have meant nothing more than the reduction of constraints. The natural landscapes, the forests, and the beaches never seemed like places I could visit without living there. I imagined travelling to beaches where the sea was warm and the sun shone all day, where the sky wasn't grey, and the air wasn't filled with a stubborn drizzle. Places where I could swim and explore and get to know my body and my mind in a new way, in a new environment. The move would let me create a new way of living, a way I kept pushing for in Cork only to find myself back where I started. But I recall now how all this sense of hope, all this sense of possibility, was initially captured by the images of new seascapes and landscapes that travel would afford me.

Years later, after I'd been living in Asia for some time, I discovered that beaches here are often polluted and crowded like everywhere else. Some only open to the public until about late September. I remember when Ryosuke and I went to Utsumi beach in Nagoya in late September. It had been a favourite hangout of ours. We approached the beach from the long narrow road leading back to the station. It was one of those typical rural Japanese roads into small towns or villages. There were old, detached houses, built the Japanese way, the timbers in the walls and roofs dried and bleached by the sea air. Metal signs rusting beside parked bicycles. There were narrow, eighties style Isuzu cars and vans parked along the way. We passed a detached house with a single tree with purple flowers in the garden. There was a large metal sign in Japanese outside the entrance. Ryosuke translated it for me. It turned out the original inhabitant of the house had been a Japanese philosopher, a member of the famous Kyoto School of Philosophy. As we both had some interest in philosophy, this find made us feel like our simple day trip to the beach had also now become a research trip or a fact-finding mission. We briefly considered what we might achieve here. How we might discover a new idea for a paper. Interview the present inhabitants. Discover they were distant relatives of this wronged philosopher who had been misrepresented as an ardent nationalist and nothing else.

- 'I don't think he was one of the famous ones. Apparently, the Kyoto School was quite big. Everyone tried to be associated with it.'

Ryosuke's words brought me back to the job at hand—our trip to the beach. When we got to the top of the low rise in the road that was leading to the beach, all of a sudden, we had a view of the vast expanse of sea before us, stretching right across our horizon. There was nothing else all around. I could even make out the grey shapes of big ships, maybe container vessels, unmoving, on the horizon. After having just been contemplating the old house and the possibility of a paper to be worked on, this sudden vision of the sea all about me, completely threw me. It filled me with fear. While we were idly chatting on the road, we had had no premonition whatsoever that we were at the edge of the land. The feeling of having the land fall away from all sides around us was also humbling and made us feel uncertain about the land beneath our feet. But soon enough we got used to it and were running along the shore together in our togs and then making the first attempt to go into the water. The water was cold, but we braved it. As we dipped our bodies under the waves the seabed seemed strangely crowded. I swam underneath the surface and peered through my goggles. There were thousands of stingrays, their grey mounds stretching away into the murky darkness like a low mountain range. We swam back to shore and crawled out of the waters. Ryosuke thought he had been stung on the back. I looked at the sallow, hairless skin of his chest and upper arms and then at his back. I

couldn't see any scratches. We decided to go back up the shore to a
small restaurant run by an old woman. Ryosuke had used it before.
It had lockers, showers and then a restaurant off to the side. The
showers were all wood panelled, like the wood panelling we had
in our house in Cork in the '80s. We met a Japanese man with
grey hair, a skinny body and an immaculate tan in the restaurant.
He was wearing white togs and his shirt was draped over the back
of the chair beside him. He was eager to talk. He had a glass of
whiskey on the table in front of him and I noticed he had a serious
scar running down his back. From the familiar way he spoke to
the old woman, we could tell he was a regular. I wondered what
such an accomplished and interesting guy was doing hanging out
here, day after day, drinking whiskey. Later, when Ryosuke lay
out the mattress for me in his apartment and we were about to
say goodnight, I found myself thinking about those moments on
the beach. When I was looking forward to the new life in Asia
from our big room in Cork overlooking the Lee and Cork city, I
could never have imagined any of this. I was filled with the light
of hope for better times ahead and the beaches became a symbol
of freedom and adventure.

The beaches in Hong Kong were smaller and more micro-
managed. To think I might be able to idle at my will on the sea
edge, untroubled by a soul, was foolhardy. Now, sitting at the pier
in Sai Kung with the threat of deadly micro-droplets from the
virus hanging in the humid sea air, with a fog gently rising off the
waters in front of me, I was aware of how nature was becoming
something we could no longer dream about in the same way.

The boy is better today. Less rumbling of mucus in his throat.
It was like a small generator going in the back room. The rumbling
in the back of the throat going all night.

Kwok-ying

The number of deaths jumped tenfold in the city of Hubei and the number of infected spiked. But numbers are pointless. No one believes them any more. They have changed the classification criteria for confirmed cases. Now they tell us they will no longer rely on test-kits but on CAT scans of the lungs and a doctor's discretion. But we all know it takes a few days for symptoms to appear. So, without numbers people will panic. If we can't have a number, we don't know how to quantify our fear. Without numbers, we can be all peoples, all sizes, all magnitudes of fear. Even quantities will soon be forgotten.

Prices didn't matter either. A box of fifty masks that ended up having only twenty-four inside could sell for sixty, 150, or even 250 dollars. No one believed the numbers because no one had believed the government for a long time, at least since the protests. And then the government insisted on having daily press conferences. No one believed these either. I kept telling Carnie. Streamed, daily press conferences kind of undid the reason for a press conference. Since the whole thing was streamed live why did the press need to be there, they asked? But the government did get everyone panicking. Panic-buying worked off the unwillingness to believe in numbers. So, when the government announced after weeks of negotiations and public mayhem over masks that they had secured the shipment of 17,000 masks for a population of 7.5 million, with each person needing at least one mask a day, the people didn't even consider believing them. There would be no point in even considering believing in those numbers.

Then there was the case of the broken sewage pipes in the stairwell of the building in Tsing Yi. It was a case of déjà vu. During SARS people had unwittingly been infected through aerosol transmission of sewage droplets from their neighbours in a public housing estate. No one knew why so many were getting infected in the building until a wily civil servant followed his nose while descending a public housing stairwell after a routine examination of the hygiene practices of inhabitants. Were they washing their hands with soap under a hot tap for at least twenty seconds? That kind of thing. Well, soon enough he discovers the source of the aerosol transmission is a rusting junction of the sewage pipes. Panic set in again. Now, with all the sewage pipes being inspected across the territory, it got people wondering about the biggest vents of all for potential aerosol transmission in the labyrinthine public and private housing estates, their own toilet bowls. Inhabitants approached their toilet bowls with extreme circumspection. No longer the scene of carefree release, the humble bowls became daily reminders of death and disease. It was only when the health department had a look at the state of the millions living in three-storey village houses where the sewage systems are not even connected to the network but instead drain freely into their own individual septic tanks, all complete with vents that occasionally vomit up the raw sewage just outside the doors and windows of the ground floor flats, that they realized they needed to stop focusing on the perils of sewage pipes. It was okay, we were advised. Find another issue, they told us. Find something less complicated to keep the public in a state of lockdown. Out of fear, of course, for public safety. One state health official reported how he liked to laugh to himself and imagine how happy Mao would have been to have lived in an age of public health and personal hygiene. Think of the stories of coercion he could have concocted related to sewage. It would have been a whole new cultural revolution.

John

The panic buying of toilet paper was not entirely unrelated. Two old ladies ripped two whole twelve-packs to shreds outside the McDonald's window this morning. My poor, sick boy has a fascination for tearing a tissue into the tiniest pieces. He forms one end of the tissue into a point and tears it slowly with the fingers of his small hands, trying to put every scrap of paper into his mouth.

Kwok-ying

Today we decided in the government that a press conference would be held at 12.45 a.m. to discuss the matter of the sewage in the public-housing estate in Tsing Yi. Having it at such an ungodly hour meant the public would either think we were mad or really cared. The next day, we were going to announce a twenty-five-billion HKD package of aid for mainland China. Sure, hadn't they already taken the majority of our surplus for the high-speed train and the Hong Kong-Zhuhai-Macau bridge? The virus would burn up the rest of the surplus. Hong Kong could no longer claim special status then. The government will today announce the provision of sweeteners for all small businesses. They will be given 1,000 HKD for the month to help tide them over. We know it is a pittance, but it might get some attention. I hear Singapore with 250 confirmed cases and twenty-three in a severe condition will soon offer all citizens a once-off 600 SG dollars cash payment. Employers have also been promised daily payments for each staff member who needs to be quarantined. We have done nothing like it yet. The last-ditch sweetener will be the general handout of 10,000 HKD to everyone. We will say it is for local businesses. Get them back on our side. Pretty soon, Hong Kong will be bankrupt. We will only have the money of mainland companies listed here. Mainland money or Vancouver money or London money. The local Hong Kongers will be wiped out. But they will have achieved their aim. They will have the arcades and the streets to themselves. They will have the MTR and the sportsgrounds back. The mainland tourists will be gone. But they will take the chains and the labels with them. There will be no shops anyone really wants to shop in. Hong Kong will be reclaimed, and they can thank the virus.

Phoebe

The talk today at our online public meeting was about the quarantine centre to be set up close to an expensive new housing development, The Mediterranean Phase III. Some apartments in the complex went for about 13.5 million HKD. The local residents were either too *gweilo* or too middle-class to protest but in the end, we got them out. We had about 500 protesters in the end. They sent in six busloads of riot police and six squad cars. An ambulance too. We walked along the coast wall shouting slogans. 'No quarantine in Sai Kung / Disease is not for everyone.' It wasn't really a slogan, but it got us going. We had buckets of hand wash and boxes of alcohol wipes. Everyone washed thoroughly at the start. Then we felt safe. Even the police batons couldn't harm us. Who fears police brutality when there is a virus to kill us all? Who fears the bloodied police baton when we have micro-droplets of coronavirus circulating throughout the air of Sai Kung? What good is quarantine when we are all already infected? Didn't one woman from Wuhan travel all the way to Shanghai, infect her entire family there and still show no symptoms herself? Aerosol transmission kind of defeats the purpose of quarantining the sick a hundred metres from the palatial Mediterranean Phase III gated community. But I need to keep my council seat. I only got elected last month on the young cute female activist ticket. Two of us got elected on the same ticket. Evelyn was more for the green movement. She even made polystyrene flowers for her election banners out of the packages for apples and oranges that the old women don't recycle. I'm the quirky, converse-wearing, shaved-headed, radical activist. We need these events since nothing ever happens in Sai Kung. It's not like Mong Kok. We'll milk this quarantine issue for all it's worth. Infected? Who knows? It's almost irrelevant now.

John

There was a letter from Hubei in the paper. A young philosophy lecturer. Stuck at home in his forty-second-storey flat with his elderly parents. They only visited to witness first-hand the success and opulence of this first-born son. Okay, he did philosophy, but now that he has the forty-second-storey flat in Rhythm Gardens he could be doing anything for all we care. Such a moving letter. So much in it to get on to him about. I'll email him and suggest a Call For Papers (CFP) for a conference on 'Surviving the Virus'. I did 'Surviving the Recession' a few years ago. Work to a theme. That's what the impact people want. Those pesky administrators at the university. They want to see the impact of our research. Or, we could call it 'Surviving the Infection'? We could have interviews and talks from the elderly and the infirm. Workshops on vulnerability. But the young philosophy lecturer in the newspaper wrote so movingly of the need to find hope. He wrote of how he and his father found three withered hydrangeas in the compost. They used earth that they had to spare and put the hydrangeas in three pots and watered them every day. They grew and flowered in the sunlight on the window sill. He wrote of how amazing and resilient life is. Of how it will find a way. I must remember this. The conference season is upon us and I need publications for the next Research Assessment Exercise (RAE).

Writing this now in the local 24-hour McDonald's, I missed the attention of a beautiful young woman who had sat beside me. Out of the corner of my eye I saw her remove her face mask. I couldn't see the face as I didn't want to turn and stare. The face would be too much now. My peripheral vision followed her movements. First, she took a soft white tissue from her Tempo pack. She spread it neatly on her lap. She wore tight, purple, hiking leggings. She withdrew the straps of the mask slowly from around her ears and gently dislodged the mask from her face. Her hands moved gracefully and with poise. I felt a kind of blood rush. The first since the virus had started, I thought. She was releasing the straps from around her ears and the tension on the mask was relaxing. She withdrew the soft fabric from the flesh around her lips ever so gently. I caught a glimpse of her face and the skin had that raw look that wounds sometimes have, wounds that are suddenly exposed to the sun. I could only see from out of the corner of my eyes. She brought it slowly down to the white carpet of tissue on her lap. The tissue resting on her lap was like a white canopy, a receptacle to receive the fleshy interior of the mask. She held the outer edges ever so gingerly as she placed it flat on the tissue. Then she folded the white tissue neatly over the mask covering it entirely. She folded it again still resting it on her lap. Then the square of tissue was put in a crisp neat little envelope and the envelope was put in a small canvas handbag.

Kwok-ying

Yes, we are chartering flights for Hong Kong residents stranded on the Dream Princess Cruise Ship docked in Japan. The volunteer health officers will determine where the patients will sit. Some will be in first class due to the severity of their condition. No meals will be served on the flights to limit contact between staff and patients. Patients will have to undergo a fourteen-day quarantine period in a centre in the Forests of Lamma. Yardlee Yeung, a forty-three-year-old mother of two who had already spent three weeks in quarantine on the Dream Princess Ship—she had only gone with other *dai ma* (a local Cantonese expression literally meaning 'big mother') to play mahjong and bet—said it was 'inhumane' that she had to be re-quarantined.

- 'I have already been in quarantine for three weeks in a first-class cabin with no windows. I will stay at home for two weeks.'

Yardlee was described by one nameless friend who wrote to the *Strait Times* as a 'social animal' and 'the life of the party'. She also had one question for the Hong Kong health authorities:

- 'Reports reveal that one patient in Vietnam was found to be infected after ninety-four days of coming into contact with someone in Wuhan. What use is a fourteen-day quarantine period?'

John

I'm back in the 24-hour McDonald's surrounded by masked faces. We just took Sam for his vaccines. Two long needles, one in either thigh. It's the delayed reaction that gets me every time. The needle goes in and out and there is silence. Then an almighty cry, an intake of breath, another silence, and then the most explosive wail of all. It must be the shock as much as the pain. I try to imagine what Sam is thinking. *Surrounded by people. Nice people. People with kind eyes. All holding me. Looking at me. I might sleep here.* Then the sharp pain in either leg. Who knows how it affects him? How it affects his image of others. Will he grow suspicious of others and begin to see their offers of help as ruses that hide their true intentions? Or maybe it will be like water off a duck's back.

I look at those around us munching on their food. I look at those still masked, waiting for their orders. Blessed are the unmasked for theirs is the freedom of breathing air directly. Two young Filipino women pass me on their way into Fusion. Unmasked, either because they don't believe the hype, or they can't afford masks. Blessed are the unmasked for they shall not fear being recognized. Blessed are the unmasked for they have the courage to walk barefaced in the early morning sunshine. Blessed are the unmasked who smell the sea air as the sun rises over Sai Kung and not their own stale breath. Blessed are the unmasked who catch the aroma of freshly-baked bolobao on the early morning sea air and not their own stale breath. Blessed are the unmasked for they shall be recognizable to the Grim Reaper when he comes looking for victims. He will pass them by in honour of their bravery.

An old woman drinks from the water-dispenser behind me which dispenses water free of charge. An old woman, barely able to walk. An old, old woman, of the kind that seem to prosper on virtually nothing in Hong Kong's meagre, social-welfare system. They get so wiry and sinewy that you end up seeing it as strength, as them being indestructible. Like those ancient slivers of the bristlecone pines you might see on a trek to the White Mountains of California. Trees so sinewy, so isolated that they could survive for millennia in rocky soil. Her brown, wrinkled skin and her purple, floral top are markers of elderly femininity here. She drops her walking stick. I see it out of the corner of my eye. I consider reaching down to pick it up, but something about the way she drinks the water, with a kind of authority, prevents me. It screams to me, in that moment, of independence. I hang back, unsure of myself. As I see her strain to pick it up, I am hit by a flood of guilt. Without the face, I'm reading people all wrong. Without the face, there is so little to go on. We are masked off from the authority of those in need. The old, old woman is now masked to the eyes again. Right up to the bridge of her nose. Her two old, glassy eyes have barely the space to peer out. Her windows to the world.

Phoebe

A cult in Korea is reported as being responsible for a super-spreader event. Fifty-three members of the Korean Shinabuchi Praise Jesus Cult have been found infected. An anti-cult pastor and researcher claims this is only half the story. The cult employs 'harvesters' he says, to steal people from traditional churches. They meet in a twenty-storey building in downtown Seoul. Married women meet on the seventh floor, married men on the eighth floor, and unmarried men and women meet on the sixth floor. They stand, shoulder to shoulder, to sing songs and pray for forty-five minutes, twice a week. The married women make household treats for all to share together with free coffee. This must happen all over Korea. They have also just published in the *Lancet* the post-mortem findings from a fifty-year-old victim of the virus. The coronavirus attacks the alveoli in the lungs. Any liver damage they say could actually be a result of medication used to treat the initial infection. The same with any heart tissue damage, they discovered. Their findings are inconclusive. It is up to us. We can't wait for science on this one. We have to fight to keep the infected away from our homes. The police will surely only fight on the side of the virus. The curfews, the rations, the ban on small gatherings and house visits have done what the police could only have wished for, they have kept everyone off the streets.

John

I think often of what we have lost. I miss smiles. We don't see them any more. Smiles used to help get me through the day. Now, the face is blank. You have to search, to have your wits about you, to catch a glimpse of a complete face. They shine like clear skies. Behind the masks you have to stare to see if the eyes are laughing or smiling. Often, in conversation, I use smiles as a sign of acceptance. I change and adapt my story accordingly. Now I'm lost. Are people smiling or looking aghast at what I say? Are they laughing at, or with, me? With the eyes alone on view there is so much ground to make up.

I spend too much time on the phone screen, trying to monitor everything. I'm checking the death count on wuhan. com. Numbers again. Can we believe any of them? I have become impervious to fear and paranoia. Everyone is infected. That is now the only way to exist. My boy hovers again on the edge of fever. He wakes up in cold sweats, the long hair at the back of his head drenched. His cheeks flushed. The mucus rattling in the back of his throat. Yes, everyone is infected. It's all we can think to avoid the fear and the paranoia.

Kwok-ying

The government has announced it is increasing its pledge from twenty-five to twenty-eight billion for the coronavirus relief fund. Legislators think it's not enough. They're arguing for single cash pay-outs. I haven't been to my office for three weeks. I get communications by email. Sometimes they send around an online circular asking us to vote on tracing measures or on the wording of the daily press releases. The daily press conferences continue but no one is tuning in. The daily stream has no viewers and I ask myself if it is like a show trial without witnesses.

Carnie doesn't seem to want our input any more. She's decided to follow orders. I've been tasked with tomorrow's Department of Health Protection press release. It's a demotion and I know it. In a funk, I took my purple Tesla out for a spin in Sai Kung last night. Scratched it reversing at speed through a line of parked cars in the taxi rank outside the 24-hour McDonald's. Some masked-up *gweilo* starts giving me grief on the Fuk Man Road beside his dirty grey jeep. I'm convinced it was that prof. from whom I took an English course for easy credits. For some reason, as he was jawing away to me, all I could think about was how far I'd fallen. From studying medicine to press releases on personal hygiene that no one reads. 'Perform hand hygiene urgently. Maintain drainage pipes properly. Dispose of soiled tissues into a lidded rubbish bin.' I have so much to offer. I could have helped find a cure for this if only I'd seen things through. I remember studying virus transmission. I remember now with something like pain those classes on how ecological changes caused by humans can really influence disease emergence. We never listened because most people don't want to know. We studied the emergence of the Nipah virus in Malaysia. Don't put fruit orchards and piggeries side by side. Fruit bats will swarm and act as reservoirs for the virus, passing it on to the pigs. A recipe for disaster. There must be more to this than press releases and contact tracing. When Laura comes back, I'll return to medicine. Either that or go all out on the gold markets.

John

Teaching has gone online. We stare for hours on end at black boxes with names across them on the screen. Everyone switches off their audio and their video. Each one of us staring for hours into black boxes to the drone of the teacher's voice. Showing videos only cuts the feed. We share documents and continue to stare into the black boxes. It's supposed to be virtual face-to-face but no one shows their faces. Even here there are masks. No one wants the camera in their cramped apartments where they live with their parents. Grandparents sucking back noodles off the same table. The sound of screaming parents or babies. None of them want a mother's, or a grandfather's, Cantonese curses broadcast to a group of sixty students all supposed to be speaking English. All competing for grades with a white teacher presiding over them like one of those stone deities staring out eternally into space on Easter Island. Sometimes, as I stare into the darkness of the screen, I try to imagine what's going on in my students' heads as my voice is piped into their family kitchens and bedrooms. *Who knows what hang-ups this white, middle-class gweilo has? Who knows what prejudices are lodged in his balding pate? Who knows how he'd weave the background noise into his marking rubric? Okay, so he doesn't want to be consciously influenced by the commotion of Cantonese going off behind me that I'm broadcasting all over the world. But he most likely will be when he thinks of me alongside the fluent, English-speaking, international-school graduates all lad-di-dah with their questions from single-occupier bedrooms. Their dreams of conservatoires and international art schools and ivy leagues. The only league I'll see is the premier league on NOW when it's back on my boyfriend's family's TV in Yuen Long.*

My colleagues are stressed out. One calls out to me across the car park as I get out of my car. She's about a hundred metres away. A mask up to her eyes. Her daughter beside her holding her hand. A mask up to her eyes as well. The white blanks of the facemasks shine out to me across the space between us. My initial reaction is to walk towards them as we speak. But then I realize I have no mask. It is in the car. I hesitate. She isn't moving. So I stop. We shout to each other across the yards of concrete. Unable to know how any of my words are being received. Simply shouting to be heard. We might as well have used semaphore. In the end, we both agree we need more masks. We move off.

A colleague sees me approaching down the corridor. He masks up. He's wearing one of those trendy black face masks. Even fighting infection can be done the right way. Even mask wearing has its highbrow and its fail culture. We talk in the corridor. He is shifty, acting as if he needs to be elsewhere urgently. I understand. We end our pleasantries. Once, I might have thought about going back to him to mention something I had forgotten. Now I don't give it a second thought. It's easier this way. Limited contact gets rid of unnecessary exchanges. It's what we wanted all along. We're happier this way. We must be thankful for small mercies. The corridor remains empty. As it should be. I sometimes wonder how we will ever face up to contact again. This is the future, they say. I walk down the long corridor feeling some kind of loss. Closed doors with the voices of teachers lecturing to different computer screens. Their accents merge as I pass. We await the passing of footsteps to emerge from our cells. No one will come out or show a face. Like those big high-tech call-centres that I worked for in Knocknaheeny. But here the students are paying top dollar to have the white face talk to their black box.

The image of the superhero fighting alone on some fiery planet comes to mind. The superheroes I teach about know nothing about the deadly virus our students are facing. The virus they face that is as deadly as kryptonite.

Yesterday we had a birthday party for my sick boy. Sue's friends came round in masks. They brought H-A-P-P-Y B-I-R-T-H-D-A-Y balloons along. Each one took some time to inflate. The only other man at the event took it upon himself to do the inflating. One of the 'Y's burst and we had to patch it up with duct tape. We strung all the letters up along our bare yellow wall and took photos. I didn't like the way their domestic helper, Delores, hung back and wanted to take all the photos, so I took a few myself and I asked her to jump in. But the amazing thing was that once all the masks were off, no one mentioned the virus for a whole four hours. We briefly had an island of reprieve from the disease talk outside our four yellow walls. It was as if we were all in quarantine from it. Our biggest emergency was dealing with Sam and his bursts of wailing. He'd go off when Kat's son, Kenny, invaded his space in the playpen, or when he just couldn't push his way forward to play with his new toys. I noticed how the three-year-old Kenny kind of took control of the new toys. He had a pyramid of bowls built within a few minutes and the little plastic Buddha sitting on top. Sam just looked on but, after a while, he started to push Kenny a little when he couldn't get his hands on the toys.

Sam got a gift of a baby xylophone and hammer. The hammer became his friend. He had no mind for the music. He just held the hammer aloft like a baby Thor and waved it around making incoherent babbling magic spells in the air. Even when I showed him how men bang things with hammers, he just took it off me and started licking the head and the handle. For a few hours we forgot there was a virus. We talked unmasked and shared sushi, strawberries, and birthday cake with a little, white-chocolate Miffy design in the centre. All across the same small table. Me being the only *gweilo*—my son, a little *gwai-zai*—I had a warmth inside me at seeing these local friends of my wife come into our flat and make it their own, transforming it into a child's party space for four hours.

Kwok-ying

We've pushed the aid package up to twenty-eight billion. It won't keep those LegCo (Legislative Council) dogs happy. Shi even wrote a personal letter to Bill and Melinda Gates thanking their foundation for the hundred-million USD contribution for research into Covid-19. Pretty awful he's reducing himself to this. Doesn't make an appearance at Politburo for months and then he's writing to US celebrities. Worse than Putin and Trump. Can you imagine Trump writing to two Chinese celebrities? Not that he'd know any. Thought he'd never stoop to this. They must be pretty shaken. The reaction to any new HK protests after this is all over will be severe. But that letter ain't gonna keep those Politburo wolves happy.

John

I've moved outside to a bench by the pier. All this writing in public has changed writing for me. I don't need to keep my head bowed any more when people pass by as I write. Jotting down notes in public has become a new normal. Like scratching an itch in public. I can also take the mask off here. The strong sea breeze coming in off the waves and the empty benches around me, fool me into thinking the chances of infection here are low. A group of Filipino women in masks take a selfie by the sea railings. They smile against the backdrop of the junks and the luxury yachts. They might never own one. Like me. But we can always get to Half Moon Bay for forty dollars. Their laughter and exuberant chatter rids them of masks for a few moments. Their naked faces are an affront to the masked Chinese and *gweilo* faces passing by.

I can't get away from the differences here. Seeing everything from two sides. 'The phoenix and the tortoise,' Rexroth calls it. Writing too 'of what survives and what perishes'. Setting out on his own epic journey, he mixes into his poem personal notes from Mallory, the mountaineer, writing his epic poem through the war years, 1940–44. Rexroth and the Beat poets would make it their mission to bring East and West together. And you fell for their gambit. Coming out here, thinking you could inspire a new kind of harmony. Now, I tell myself that here, from my pier-side bench in Sai Kung, with everyone masked to the gills, it's much harder to tell East and West apart. 'It's worse than wartime,' my mother tells me when I call her on the phone. Yes, that's it. The virus is the great unifier this time. It sees us all only as one.

Phoebe

They say the new quarantine centre in Fotan doesn't even have tiles on the floor. Children have been taken ill coughing up the concrete dust. They say there is under-reporting of cases and even of deaths. It's no surprise. The police are experts at under-reporting. What about those killed in Prince Edward during the protests? That young girl they claim walked naked to her death by drowning in the sea in Tseung Kwan O? She would have had to walk about a kilometre. Today, I walked into the new Covid-19 Test Centre in Ma On Shan. Wanted to see how the system works. Pretended I had food poisoning. Had to pass people in hazmat suits at the entrance and navigate the cordon sanitaire and its circus. There were two patients in the whole centre. No one is going to hospitals or clinics. They're staying at home no matter how they feel. Why book yourself into a cramped ward when there is no cure?

At night, I take photos of the empty streets of Hong Kong and upload them to Instagram with captions. Radical street photography I call it. Sometimes in English, sometimes in Chinese. Tonight, I took a shot of an empty Boundary Street. A street marking a disappearing line of identity. A line from Leung Ping Kwan came to mind in English, 'Finding the promised land and expanding the imagined border.'

John

There is to be no let up. Yesterday the Chinese authorities in Hubei retracted a decision to ease the lockdown. It seems they'd forgotten to count 150 new deaths for the day. Not exactly restoring our confidence, you could say. My wife hasn't left the house for a week. I'm reduced now to going out before sun up. At about 5.30 a.m., I hit the streets armed with disinfectant spray, hand wash, mask and glasses. In the dark, figures emerge out of the blackness, indistinct. Most of these nightwalkers are unmasked for some reason. Makes them look even more dangerous. Distances are pronounced in the dark. I pass a group of teenagers all dolled up from the night before. Two girls in short skirts or long sweat shirts and tight bobs. A young guy in a full suit stands with them by the sea wall. One of the unmasked girls halloos good morning to me and all I can do is pant heavily as I pass. I get the diminishing essentials in the local market. Toilet paper's all gone so I'm now onto old newsprint I hoard and have hoarded. There is still rice and some of the expensive western biscuits half-coated with seventy per cent dark chocolate. I joke to Sue they'll be the last product on the shelves when the virus bites. She doesn't eat them any more.

I have come down with a whole bunch of mouth sores. Lesions I think they're called. Can't take anything even remotely tepid. I let my coffee go stone cold. The little guy has fever again. We'll try to get out next month after my cheque comes in. I hear some cheques have been stopped. I'm not thinking about that. I hear some airlines are still flying out here. The diplomats have nearly all left.

I remember watching *10 Years After* in Hong Kong and crying at the destruction imagined down the tracks. But even dystopian science fiction requires some belief in a future. I had never realized how individual one's view of the future is. We don't all view it in a single, collective way. We carry our secret histories and our secret futures inside like precious memories. Once these futures are twisted or threatened, we don't know where to look. We panic and lose our bearings. I gave up looking when the government policed our imagined futures.

Some poet friends met up for what we called our 'last hurrah'. We knew it would be a last drink. Each one of us brought along three favourite poems to read. A schoolboy prank but it got us reading again. I broke down half way through the 'Lake Isle' and couldn't be revived until after I'd stepped out for ten minutes. I still heard my father's voice in my ears reciting it in front of the old house in Cork. That Cork sunshine which I hadn't ever stored away because I always thought I could return to it whenever I wanted. It's funny how the most familiar places and faces refuse to conform to the work of memory.

A sixty-something American guy who'd met Rexroth and Carver told us a story about Rexroth's final reading and how he banged out the rhythm of his poem on the desk using his old wallet. I launched into an impromptu response on how at least we were keeping the word alive. The word that we all live for. But then it hit me harder. Were any of our words getting out? No one read them beyond our small groups.

At night there is a silence that descends on the village. A deep silence. Like the ocean at low tide. I pass through the narrow lanes and see windows lighted behind closed curtains. Street lamps send out a clinical yellow glow that now only reminds me of a hospital ward. The lonely comfort of street lamps at night can at least grant me the reassurance of direction and of destinations plotted and lighted. It's in the darkness beyond the range of the lamp light that I feel vulnerable. Rumours abound of families burying their own dead. Why go to the hospitals, they say? Why go to the hospitals when there is no cure and when it means quarantine for you and your family, for your friends, for anyone you ever met or ever sat beside. Would they ever talk to you again? So, the yellow and off-white lights we see behind drawn curtains on the balconies of village houses burn too in our minds and in our imaginations. What stories do they illumine?

My sister tells me not to go back home to Cork. She's locked in on her own in London. She says our parents are under lockdown and they're doing okay. But they need someone on the ground. They're in their mid-eighties and no nurses are calling in on anyone now. My sister says it's too dangerous. You can't go back. I tell her none of us are infected here but it's no good. I hear it too sometimes when I call my mother. The fear. How distance breeds distrust of the numbers. I say there are more cases in Cork than Hong Kong. But this is how it starts. Once doubt is seeded. The unquestioned acceptance of the distance between us and the impossibility of bridging it. Even your own mother is too afraid to see you. She'll see you all right, on the phone, but getting any closer is the hard part. I never imagined that the face-to-face would become such a privilege. Even if I beg, which I'm not going to do, I can't shake this fear.

Europe too is teetering. In Asia they bought up all the facemasks and now there aren't enough to ship back there. My own brothers were sending me boxes without a thought for how they might soon need them for themselves. We never imagined the queues at chemists on Tottenham Court Road when we queued on Fuk Man Road.

Our sick boy keeps us up all night. He plays with straps and cords from my bags and headphones. Put a toy in front of him and he has no interest. Maybe he can feel it screaming 'I'm a toy'? My wife has come down with fungus on her toes. On top of everything.

Stocks have suffered their worst day since 2011. Down 4.4 per cent. The US has an outbreak of 800 in California, but they only have 200 test kits.

I imagine how life and even love might prosper here. I think of the students I've taught who are now all cooped up at home. I call one whom I've asked to do a talk for me on anime and manga. He says he'll do it. It's all online now. He says he'll do it in the voice of an alien who comes to earth to feast on corpses. I hear him giggling uncontrollably, at the other end of the phone, as he tells me.

We're reading Shelley this week in class. All his talk about death. Destroyer and preserver he calls the wind. Predicting his own watery death in his 'The Spirit of Solitude'. Even 'Ozymandias' is about dead kings and the passing of old orders. He could only write if death had a part in it. We're back there now, back with the pervasive sense of death. But we're not calling on the wind or on Keats's nightingale to distract us from death. Today we want the details, the numbers, the science.

Phoebe

Reports come in on US websites saying the virus was manufactured. Of course, the stories are kept out of China. If it was manufactured, then there's only one place it happened. But it won't stop the trade talks. It won't stop Lim jailing peaceful activists. Not a chance. Yesterday I watched a Netflix documentary to get my mind off the virus. The *Pharmacist*. About some American pharmacist whose son dies from opiates. He researches the decades of state-sanctioned selling of opiates to vulnerable youths. The state bankrolling the death of thousands of its own people. It got me thinking. Is there any difference between that and what some in the US are saying happened here? Engineer what you call a 'natural disaster' to cover up any sense that a GDP slowdown or an economic decline are down to policy. The government can now blame the fall in productivity on a virus, not its own authoritarian policies. Genius really. Not much of a risk. A slight bump in popularity ratings. Sacrifice maybe 5,000 of your own people. Chiefly the elderly and the infirm. A drop in the ocean in a country of 1.4 billion. A face-saving, global agenda. Then come back strong in the state media as the benevolent ruler who stood up and contained the virus.

John

This morning there was the most beautiful sunrise over Sai Kung. The orange ball of the sun above the shimmering sabre of orange light along the waves reaching back to me. It only shines with such brilliance in the first sun up. It only lasts about twenty minutes in all its brilliance and in each second of this time it is fading into daylight. The sun worshippers of old have their brethren today. As I jog on the strip of grass by the sea wall, Ma On Shan rising on one side, the sea breaking on the other, two men with radios blaring stand on the upper deck of the Sai Kung Jockey Club Golf Island Car Park. They are here for the first sun up every morning. They throw their arms out doing repetitive Chinese calisthenics. When I first arrived, I couldn't see them standing back in the shadows on the upper deck. In the semi-darkness, I thought the voices came from a radio someone had lost in the long grass. Now I see it's the two old men stretching as they stare out at the sunrise. They call out to passers-by walking along by the sea wall 'Jo San! Jo San!' The mask-wearing, shadowy figures call back as if they had expected the greeting. Now I can see the silhouettes of the men on the deck. It's the distance that allows them to talk. Sometimes the conversation goes further. 'Jo San. Sic Jo. A good morning all right. Don't forget your radio. Don't forget your car!' For a moment, once again, there is no virus. The sun has brought us together. That's the way it is for all of us now. Only able to communicate from the shadows and with distance between us.

The first brilliance is a deep orange glow. I remember the footage NASA released of those high-resolution close-ups of the sun's surface. It looked like a glowing, heaving cauldron of small coals. Or a radiating ball of small worm-like ghosts squirming in alien temperatures. To think that it is the cause and sustainer of everything I see here, as well as their potential destroyer. We're back with Shelley again. Even the light that allows me to perceive this shot I'm trying to line up is only a result of that which I'm trying to shoot. A self-reflective shot. Even the light metre on the screen showing the shot I'm trying to take of the father of all light sources only takes me back to that big old sun. To think that everything I see, and all the ways I try to capture it, are only references to the same thing, is almost infuriating. All roads lead back to that sun, that same sun they're saying will save us all from the virus come April or May. Only to burn us to a crisp a few decades later. My efforts to escape it all by capturing a moment of beauty on my dawn walk along the promenade only return me to that life. All the time we spend trying to flee the chaos and the destruction by capturing these moments only leads us back to the cause of it all and to the limited nature of our own perspective. There is no skyhook upon which to ground our theories they used to tell me when I was in college, but no, it's the opposite, there is nothing but skyhooks through which to understand what we see. We only ever keep going back to what and where we are. But it's the suspension of disbelief that matters. Suspend our disbelief in what keeps promising to take us elsewhere rather than straight back to ourselves. And beauty seems to do it. The beauty we never teach or know or even know how to access any more. Faces were a spur to the contemplation of beauty but now they are gone. Beauty is the flower of winter for the Chilean novelist Roberto Bolaño. It's the hardest thing to see as most things only mask it in this age of concealment.

I took great comfort now in the fact that I still wanted to stop for a shot at beauty. It is being destroyed by the very image of beauty I frame. Without a reference point for beauty, we are left floundering. Does each one of us become a measure of beauty?

Because we're worth it? But that's not it either and you know it. I need to rediscover the beauty in others too not just in myself. I must look for it more in Sue and in my sick boy. And where is that woman who took her mask off beside me last week in McDonald's? I could start with her. Only for the sake of beauty. I'd know her if I saw her again. Wasn't she that local politician I spoke to on the day of the election? The one with the shaved head and the converse? The one I voted for?

Kwok-ying

The government has announced the suspension of all schools until at least 20 April. It's ideal. People are afraid to congregate. Serves them right. No one is protesting. The government couldn't have dreamed for a better Divine Intervention. Isn't that what it's called? All that time wasted on that bloody English course. What was the name again? Ah yes. Literature and Religion. Literature and Anything. Literature and Fried Eggs. And the professor's name? Ah yes. John Ryan. Scatterbrain. Selling us a whole pack of lies. The only damn thing I remember from the course is that phrase. Divine Intervention. For some reason it stayed with me. That's what the virus is. And not because it stops people meeting and hanging out. Giving us social distancing. It also gives us the space to arrest the Kingpin Culprits of the Protests. Those left-wing media guys. We couldn't touch them while people were out protesting. Now we'll swoop and only the lunatic fringe will come out. Get them all locked up. Then they'll forget. Look at that Occupy Guy still in prison in Sai Kung. Never a word anywhere about him. I even hear he gets no visitors, except for his partner. An academic too. These sad, brainwashed loners. Now no one's got the balls to come out. And they call themselves hardliners. Pah! The lining in my boxers, or skinny jeans, is harder. Sure, the worst they can do is throw rotten plants around in the chamber. The police walk straight up to their front doors and they come willingly. 'Put me in prison. It's better than this paranoid wife I'm living with. She won't even let me touch her or the kids. Says it's all bad karma. The result of what I started. I have to wear plastic gloves in my own home.' They feel the only place to escape this region-wide quarantine paranoia is in prison. No one cares about prisoners. So long as they're not infecting anyone other than themselves. And for that we just cut visiting. Best thing for all of us is to lock ourselves up in our own cells and throw away the keys.

Phoebe

These long months of protests, then of campaigning for the elections, and now the weeks of being cooped up at home. I've been talking to my counsellor again on Zoom about depression. She tells me I must turn off my rational brain sometimes. Look for the emotional, she says. Let my feelings go. Not much chance they can travel very far from here. Thing is I've always found love in my activism. In my campaigning, debating, arguing, fighting. I've convinced myself life is too serious for anything else. We have a city to save after all. Love? I've masked myself off. Cut the connection. We can't let emotion in. As soon as we do, they'll spot the weakness and exploit it. Turn it against us. Then we're lost. I wasn't always like this, I guess. I remember in school there was a girl I liked to be with. Wing Man and I sat on the swings in the playground, talking for hours. Never felt like going through the motions. Since then, it's been campaign, fight, win. Look for the weakness in any argument they give you. Accept nothing at face value. Never rest. Spot the bullshit and call it out. Never let it pass. Emotion only gets in the way. Maybe now I need some of it? Maybe there is something in it I overlooked? No matter how destructive the government is, if we let them take our capacity and our desire for love, then what are we fighting for at all? Will freedom be worth anything to us at all when it eventually comes? Will we even be able to recognize it when we see it?

John

I heard the running track was open today. First time in two months. No new case yesterday and no new death for two weeks. People are holding their breath. Behind their masks, mind you. There is a sense the worst is over. The cotton trees are blooming. Those red shots of colour against the grey bark and the branches reaching out like arms with cupped hands and long, spindly fingers. Hero trees they call them. We need heroes today. It's still raging all over Europe, but here it's slowing.

I made it to the entrance to the running track. They had barriers all down the middle dividing an entrance stream from an exit stream. A woman sat at a desk at the head of the entrance channel. She was gloved and masked. She pointed to a sign. It read 'Sanitation Mat'. I couldn't see anything. I looked down and there was a small, bright red doormat at the beginning of the entrance channel. The woman couldn't speak English and my Cantonese wasn't good enough to ask 'what do I do with the Sanitation Mat?' so I stepped on it and wiped my runners a few times back and forth for good effect and to make it look like I took it all seriously. I wondered what good it did. Sanitize the soles of my runners? Possibly the least likely place on me to be the source of contagion. But I knew we had to feel we were doing something. There has to be some ritual between complete closure and regular opening hours.

When I got onto the track, I saw some of the familiar faces. There was the guy who jogged real slow with headphones. I passed the guy with the greying hair who I always took for a civil servant. He not only jogged on the outermost lane of the track but also around the perimeter of the jagged pieces of track at the corners that spilled out well beyond the confines of the outermost lane. He milked ever last yard from each lap. There was the woman who always seemed to speed up when I lapped her. I passed them all for the first time in many weeks. It was then that I noticed they were all walking on the track instead of jogging. I got a chance to see their expressions too as I passed them for, as I jogged by, I made sure to look back at them in case they wanted to share with me their exuberance at having the track back. But words failed me at the last moment. Each one of them looked far from elated. Instead, they looked worse for wear, even a little pale and sullen, with their greying hair a little more unkempt than I remembered. I began to wonder if the open track suddenly made them feel that the ordeal of jogging every morning was no longer denied them. The daily task of keeping up, of fending off unfitness, beckoned once again. 'Why couldn't the track stay closed so that we had a reason not to take part in this daily farce?' I could almost feel their looks scream it at me.

Then we heard they were closing all public facilities again due to a second wave.

Phoebe

The virus provided us with so much certainty. There was 'No Running', no use of the sportsground, no working in the office, no riding in the rush-hour MTR. All of a sudden, life had the clear guidelines I'd longed for that allowed me to be myself, to even find myself. Okay, for a few days, I did miss the camaraderie of the council office. But pretty soon, I adapted. Now, with the first wave over and things returning to normal, I started to see the weeks of isolation that the virus lockdown had afforded me as a glorious missed opportunity. How close I felt to something important. With time standing still and the daily grind of work revealed for what it was, I longed again for a second chance. Couldn't you give me back the hiatus a second time? I promise this time I'll know how to manage it. I'll discover the person I'm meant to be. I was so close. All the time spent on caring for parents, touching them, hearing their stories. All the time spent making homemade facemasks and alcohol wash, baking and reading. Something inside was changing and beginning to take hold. I rediscovered a part of me that I had kept under for so long just to get a salary. Give me the time over and I'll show you I can make the most of it. Give it to me again and I promise you I'll have a living concocted for myself at the end of it. But no, there was not going to be a second virus any time soon. The government would get us all back on track so the routine would again seem what we were made for. It would be our saving grace. Wasn't it the Lion Rock Spirit? Get us all back on track and loving it so that the protesters might be vilified for ever challenging it or disrupting it. They would make us see that

Hong Kong was its routine and nothing else. We would all take up our tools with renewed vigour and even a sense of reverence. The gods save anyone who threatened to take it from us again.

* * *

Phoebe

'**D**ead Inside.' That's what it read. On her hoodie. She was walking ahead of me to the bus stop. Tight black leggings, the hoodie with the words 'Dead Inside' and then the facemask up to her eyes. There was a whole new industry around death today. People had come so close. It had marked them. They could now proudly wear 'Dead Inside'. People toyed with the idea more. They wore their trauma on the outside. They could joke about it. Was this big business cashing in on people waking up to the reality of death? It was everywhere but we liked to shut it out. Quarantine it. If we didn't talk about it, we were obsessed by it. We never stopped watching zombie flicks. But this was unreal death. It was Death on Ice. I read 'Dead Inside' as she walked before me as this ironic nod to the fact that we were all dead inside if we didn't let Death In.

I looked around me in the 24-hour McDonald's. People needed this space. All our efforts to reclaim the streets but McDonald's, the biggest fast food corporation on the planet, was the only place you could walk into without bouncers or security hassling you and sit down unbothered for as long as you liked, for days if you wished. It would probably change pretty soon, but for now I was lovin' it. And you could sip as much free warm water as you liked too. There was this sense of 'sanctioned loitering' about the place. Free piped music too. Free toilets. It was for many a home away from no home. We all knew about the hundreds of homeless living in McDonald's because they had nowhere else to go. So, the man in front of me tucking into a fish fillet across from his daughter with the cup of sweetcorn was a sign that most just got on with it. The *Dai Ma* chomping on fries talking about the best alcohol wipes. The woman in front of me who watches Korean drama on her phone with her deluxe hot cakes. A plump woman who looked a little schoolboy-like with her cropped hair but who I could tell was probably in her forties. The old woman in the wheelchair by the window looking out on the passers-by, chomping on her hash brown. Wheeled in every morning by her sixty-something son and left by the window. Each day he asks someone to watch over his mother. 'I'm just going next door. Could you keep an eye on her for a minute?' They had survived death. They were far from dead inside. But they were marked by the death that had ravaged their community. These were the people I was elected to serve. I felt it now in the aftermath more than ever. This connection with them.

I saw that *gweilo* in there again too, the one writing by the window. Did he speak to me on election day? Sat beside him last time. He's spotted me looking. Hold the stare.

John

The routine couldn't save me in the end. The feeling of pointlessness was hard to shake. It becomes almost tactile when you persist in doing what you're doing without meeting anyone. It's like a cold, metallic taste that gets to the roots of your teeth and makes your head freeze. Descending the stairs from the roof of our building to the space outside our door, I suddenly had a bird's eye view of how we were living. The mess was clear from here. Never so clear close-up. Shoes pitched all over the landing, stray shreds of dried grass from the soles of old runners, old shoe boxes discarded willy-nilly and lying open, the lids thrown all over the steps. It seemed to sum up my dull sense of emptiness. But we would have to continue. In looking back at my life before, I was beginning to realize how even the most fleeting of meetings are accumulated unawares to give us a sense of our humanity. The casual glance or smile was like a relational photosynthesis. Robbed of this, my leaves dried up and shrivelled away to nothing, leaving dry, brittle bark and branch.

On the days I left Sue and Sam at home, I would go into the department corridor for the odd book or to teach a class online. Walking down the corridor, I'd hear the teachers lecturing to their computer screens in their offices. Capsule teaching, I called it. I realized most of my colleagues might prefer it this way. Avoid any possibility of human contact or interaction, the thing most good academics were uneasy about.

Today the 24-hour McDonald's was packed. The second wave rules were not here yet. We were enjoying a brief reprieve. Standing room only. Queues for individual seats. Groups of Filipino women milled around desperate for seats on their one day off in the week.

I had had a long Skype call the night before with a former PhD student. He's about ten years younger than I am and he just got on the job market. Rick's holed up in Wuhan with his Chinese wife. They can't leave their building together. Every three days, one of them can leave to buy essential provisions. They go to the local market, hand in their order, and the supplies are passed out to them on a long stick. Social distancing is extreme in Wuhan, but on Skype I was suddenly staring at him unmasked, up close in his sitting room. He showed me round his apartment. It had flashy new fittings and fancy ceiling mouldings like many of the new apartments in China. The rooms were bigger than here, but when he showed me the living room it looked empty and the furniture old-fashioned. The bad lighting created a cold feeling that no amount of ceiling design could dispel. Rick was now staring right at me. From a world of no faces, all of a sudden, I had a face taking up the whole of my screen. His skin was pale and pasty from having been indoors for months. He had that intense frown I had always associated with him. I put it down to him being smart as well as interested in research. But this time the shadows across his face made the frown look like it was making parts of his forehead protrude. I asked him how his work was going. I had been struggling to find any kind of emotional intensity for my work. My sick boy took up most of my hours after work and most of my mental energy too.

It seemed the virus only made the isolated intensity of academics more pronounced. Rick was comparing programming to creative writing in his new paper. He had been reading up for weeks on the history of computer programming and creativity. I admired his dedication. Staring at him in the low-resolution monochrome light, his furrowed brow and his intense stare revealed to me for a moment what was wrong with my profession. It celebrated isolated intensity. He never spoke to me of any practical benefits of his work but the intensity with which he spoke about his work could have powered a small town. He spoke of top journals, publication counts, citation and impact scores. Mostly numbers. I told myself it was the stage he was at. We all went through it. The only difference going through it now, during lockdown, was that lockdown made the isolated intensity seem normal. Quarantine, lockdown, and the virus made it all feel normal, like this was how we should be and had to be to get through. Wasn't everyone feeling their own version of isolated intensity? It was almost as if the academic's world had become everyone's world. The world where too much isolated intensity seemed abnormal was gone. This abnormal environment, this world of social distancing and of staying indoors, this online, virtual world was now the one all academics had to write for and research for. The academic could now emerge into the kind of world he had always secretly craved. There was no one in the corridor to stop him to ask him how his work was going? No casual conversation over lunch on campus could help shake his convictions. No immediate face-to-face reaction from students—living, breathing, embodied students— on hearing about his new research mid-lecture could shake his isolated intensity. No one gave him that dispirited, unimpressed, sometimes aggressively hostile look that made him question his new ideas. There were none of the usual checks on the isolated, self-congratulatory intensity of the academic. He became a free-floating signifier for anything. With my sick boy crying night and day and the virus keeping me locked in with the 24-hour McDonald's my only outlet, I felt it was only a matter of time before the scaffold for isolated academic intensity disappeared and a world of desperate need emerged. I needed to wake up and prepare myself. How would I cope with trying to understand this level of need? How would I be able to help if I didn't understand where they were coming from? Isolated self-congratulatory intensity was only going to prevent me from learning. I needed to stop writing so I could start talking, listening and feeling. My boy would help me. He would help me understand need. I needed to look up from my pad and not only stare momentarily outside the window at the trees and passers-by beyond the masked face facing me but also to look into the eyes of that face and try and talk. It was time to put down the pencil. My book is closed, I read no more.

Phoebe

They do death differently in China. Reports say a new quarantine centre in China just collapsed killing ten people. It was only built in 2018. Talk about going from the frying pan into the fire. Can they get anything right? China is already finessing the image of itself as lockdown saviour of the world. Who can lockdown like us? We have lockdown down. We own lockdown. They're pushing reports about how Chinese scientists are almost ready to use a vaccine in emergency cases. Clinical trials? Why, of course. We tested some rats and they survived. We even tested it on pangolins! Who's now checking their ethical standards? Their test results? They are selling lockdown to other countries. Twenty million masks to Italy. So what if they treat their dead differently to the West? Haven't we long known they treat their living differently? There will be no public enquiry into the thousands of dead. No change of tack. The biggest lockdown of people in history worked. Further proof of the value of authoritarianism. Liberal newspapers are already calling for authoritarianism to be reconsidered. Opinion pieces deliberate on what might be achieved if it could only be managed better. Spin the positives to a vulnerable, paranoid international public. They'll grasp at anything. Anything to get their footie back on the TV. Anything to have toilet rolls back in their supermarkets. Death is done differently in China. No inquest. Get people back to work and then spin the narratives. Burn the bodies in the 24-hour crematoria. Throw them into refrigerated trucks. Imprison the nay-sayers. But get out the vaccine out. Only then will you snatch victory from the jaws of defeat.

I saw an old Italian man on TV. He was saying the worst part of it all is that there are no funerals. The priests come and say a few prayers and that's it. You spend your entire life on the Mediterranean diet. You wear Italian handmade shoes. You've always had a perfect tan and waistline. Then you're burnt without ceremony because of infection. He looks directly at the camera.

- 'They tell you this virus doesn't discriminate. I spent my life discriminating and look where it got me? It's in all the places my friends used to travel they tell us. Northern Italy, Switzerland, New York. We never hear much about the South of Italy, about the Southern States of America, about Africa.'

II

Hong Kong
April-May 2020

Phoebe

I remember the day I got the call from the Government Health Bureau telling me I had been in direct contact with someone who tested positive for Covid-19. I had just got to my office in Sai Kung town. I could barely walk when I got the call. My chest was heaving. I was sweating buckets. The quarantine place wasn't so bad in the end, and it was just down the road. Right beside where my friend bought an expensive new apartment last year for eleven million HKD, in that new complex they called The Mediterranean! As my symptoms aren't severe, they've told me to stay here. If they get worse, they'll send me to a hospital. My temperature keeps peaking so they won't let me out. I've been 'cured' twice but then the next test result came back and I still had the infection, so it was another fourteen days inside.

Kwok-ying

Carnie finally wore a face mask. I've been telling her since it all kicked off. She thought it would contravene the Mask Ban she brought in for the protests. Serves her right. Never listens. Sure, we didn't see her for months. One KOL whom I follow tweeted she had extradited herself to Wuhan to meet Shi. We need someone strong in here to sort this out. Shi was wearing facemasks meeting the public back in January. Avoiding handshakes, shouting up to waving residents isolating in their apartments. But no, she would never visit residents in Sheung Shui or Jordan right now. Sooner have her hair done.

I got the bad news last week. The Positive Test. Someone in here got it, but the air is so stale, it took weeks to circulate. I still have to work from here in quarantine. Where can we go to be ill when we're all online? Where can we go to truly self-isolate? Still have the laptop and all my passwords. It's getting crowded in here, mind you. Whole housing estates, even Royal Ascot, have now been taken over by the quarantine department. The government will never admit they've lost control. Most people now avoid hospitals. Why tell the authorities you're infected when you, all your family, and anyone you ever met will end up here, in quarantine. The more time I spend here, the more I realize that quarantine is the new normal. The ones who aren't in here yet are the exceptions. It's one big decoy. Don't do anything in case you get infected. You follow the rules, live like a hermit, still get infected, then end up being sent here where it's impossible to live like a hermit. We're all incubating the virus at home and then the quarantine zones are spreading all the time. We all know we've lost. And even though we've lost and it is everywhere, we still feel locked up. Travel everywhere is impossible and you're hit with self-quarantine if you do get out and come back. And the thing is they will never relax some of these changes. Especially now since our top epidemiologist, Chan Lok Man, has come on TV saying the virus will only be back stronger in the autumn and winter with no serious vaccine in sight before then. This is only the entrée, the appetizer, he said. He actually chuckled when he said it. On National TV. These guys spend so long inside crunching numbers, it all becomes a game.

Phoebe

We were the long-tails. The long-term, low-grade cases of infection. Some of us had symptoms now for over three months. They didn't know what to do with us. Our tests kept coming back positive, but our symptoms didn't worsen. Sometimes they even disappeared, only to rise up again the next week. Some had lingering sore throats or raging headaches. Others had lost their sense of smell and taste. It didn't much matter in here. The rooms and corridors only smelled of alcohol cleanser and the food only tasted of low-grade congee.

They moved us to our own quarantine centre on Lamma, and the rules were more relaxed. Since some of us had been inside for two or three months with no human contact, they worried about our mental state. They couldn't just leave us in our rooms all the time. As there were so many of us now, so many long-tails, they had to find a way to get us out of our rooms for part of the day. So, they installed a Quarantine Coffee Dock. Can you believe it? I walked the concrete compound and sometimes visited the 24-hour limited-seating Coffee Dock that some wealthy property magnate had asked them to install. The places big business can reach! They kept it open all hours with stringent rules on temperature checks, masks and distancing and they get us to stagger our visits.

* * *

I have been seeing that *gweilo* in here a lot over the last few weeks. I'm sure he's the same one from the McDonald's in Sai Kung. No longer writing. Can't work out if he's one of us or one of them. He spoke to me the other day as I passed, and I almost jumped. Even with the two of us fully masked and two metres apart. Strangers don't talk to each other these days. He laughed, then apologized.

- 'I'm sorry I didn't mean to shock you.'
- 'No, it's my fault. I'm just paranoid. This virus has made us all paranoid.'
- 'What are you in for?'
- 'Well it's not for rioting!'
- 'You must be a long-tail like me?'
- 'Yes, I'm hoping to bankrupt the place.'

I see him there most days now. For some reason it makes me feel secure seeing him there.

John

I've been in quarantine now for weeks. Seen the full range of camps. From Fotan to Sai Kung. And they're moving me again soon. A work colleague somehow got it. It must have been the department toilets. Or maybe the pantry. I've racked my brain about what I could have done differently. We're what they call the long-tails. Those with low-grade, long-term infection. Our symptoms vary but they're never severe. They don't want us in the hospitals. So they keep us out here, in the wilderness of Sai Kung. Reports say they might move us, long-term cases, out to Lamma. Hear they've even installed a small Quarantine Coffee Dock in the compound out there. Big business getting its fingers in everywhere. Truth be told, the inside was starting to look a lot like the outside. The virus was making the space outside quarantine look like the real quarantine space. The quarantine was sucking everything in like a vortex. The quarantine was taking over but the world in here was fast becoming the only world.

It's funny how the events of the past come back to haunt you when you're suddenly barred from doing the kinds of things that allowed those events to happen. They come back not only as moments from your life but as a long-departed way of life. More and more I find myself recalling the slightest detail nostalgically. As if it will never be repeated. The embracing and the handshakes. The long kisses into the early morning beside an old cassette player. The song 'Linger' by the Cranberries playing over and over in a small cottage on Magazine Road in Cork. I'm not one to give myself up to memories. I don't like to spend time looking into the moving images of memory to get back the taste, the shape of the hand, the feel of the lips, but here with so much ruled out, I want to remember what it was like. How physical we were. Thinking nothing of sharing lips, tongues, saliva and caresses for hours. Until the taste of the lover seemed like our taste, until the smell of the lover on our clothes was left to linger for days. The disappointment when the perfume could no longer be smelled on the back of the hand or on the small hairs of the forearm. In quarantine now I know we'll never get this back. Never again will we even shake hands with the same abandon. And yet there is relief too at what we have given up. The petty work talk. The daily grind. The pointless drive for targets and goals.

Trouble is I can still teach from quarantine. They put in a high-speed connection. Sick days are hard to come by in quarantine. Online almost feels normal at times. It's like a one-sided conversation with a group of old invisible acquaintances when you switch off your video and give yourself up to it.

After a long online class or call with a student, I walk out into the corridor and for a moment everything is normal. There is no virus. Then it hits you. You remember everything is not normal. You see the empty corridor and you remind yourself why. It hits like a sudden remembrance of a looming deadline or presentation. It's a sense of pressure from some overwhelming burden. It's something you know you can't shake. You know you will walk around with it rattling around in your head until something—a quiet moment with a coffee, a moment of care for your sick child—will make you forget it again for an instant.

I call my mother, and she says it is all God's punishment. Not in a painfully evangelical way but more in a matter-of-fact way. Like its common knowledge. I agree with her as I sometimes feel it myself. I think of those childhood stories from the Bible. The plague of locusts. The pictures in our Children's Bible. How reassuring it would be if it was God's punishment. It would be a sign that a moral force prevailed. That God was saying enough is enough, that He was telling us to stop our evil ways. But I was always more impressed and captivated by the fictional stories of childhood than by those in which God stepped in to offer a resolution. I didn't have the resilience anymore to follow my divine questions through to the end. I preferred to leave the matter open so that when I instinctively called on prayer later that day, I could do it with a little more heart.

Kwok-ying

We are rolling out the news stories for the new policy— 'Proclaim to World How China is the Saviour of a World Infected by C' or PWCSWC for short. I'm covering the attacks on other world leaders. I have a quote from a Chinese health official: 'How can you believe in a leader who cannot make his people wear masks?' The guy actually said this. At a 'meet the people' session in Wuhan. We're running with it. No leader can wear a mask like Shi or NLCWMS for short. It's doing well. And a new line on how well the new Carnie carries off mask-wearing. It's always COVID-19, never coronavirus and never mention Wuhan or Hubei.

Sue

I decided I'd had enough when John ended up in quarantine. He has been in there now for months. And now he's talking about going back to Ireland to help his mum and dad when he gets out. Does he have any idea? What does he think we are? Pieces of furniture he can pick up and discard whenever he feels like it? So, I took Sam with me and moved back in with Mom. It's been tough in lockdown for months with him anyways. Before any of it, he was spending all his time writing that garbage in McDonald's of all places. I mean, what's he thinking? They'll think he's one of the new homeless.

He doesn't even know what he is to us or how he was my brave lover. A wave of pain passes through me when I remember those days. Seeing him smiling the morning he ran out to me in the Hong Kong midday sun in the cheap sandals, their buckles untied, his feet slamming down on the concrete driveway of the village to keep the sandals from flying off. Me turning to him in the sunshine in the red dress he had bought me the week before. That smile of pure unadulterated fun, with not a strain of irony, or arrogance, or tolerance breaking out across his face. Like happiness itself. Had he ever smiled like that in the last three years? When would he smile like that again? When would I feel like that again? My face turning to him and everything fresh and bright in the sunlight with the stinkbugs croaking in the fig trees that sheltered the overflow from the septic tanks. My voice coming to him in the early morning air, 'my brave lover, my brave lover.' He had braved the concrete in his sandals for me. But he has forgotten that bravery. Can he ever be so brave again to give up on his work for us? To give up his ghost of a dream?

He's no different from the rest of them when it comes down to it. All the white men I've met are pretty much the same. And why are English teachers so stuck up? It's not as if they teach anything useful. The snobbier they are, the higher they climb. Sweating, balding men with their ruddy skin and bloodshot eyes. Marching up and down between the rows of desks, showing PowerPoint slides of the faces and poems of more white men. Accents I can only ever half understand. So nervous or hung-over, they fill the slides with text and theories the students never have time to read. None of them are any good apart from that one guy who used to make us feel something for the work. He was always going on about sex and gender. About the male gaze, the phallus, fetishes, homophobia, camp, cross-dressing, transsexuals. I'd never heard of these things in English before then. When I told my friends in engineering or nursing, they just shouted *chiseen* (crazy) and asked why I was wasting good money and my best years on it. But it got into my head. I never looked at trains and tunnels, mirrors, columns, handbags, and old men the same way again. Go to college to read about love poetry and you come out thinking love is only a performance and sexuality is something you can put on and take off like makeup.

I can't forget how he learnt Cantonese slang to impress me. He couldn't get over himself when he learnt that the Cantonese for cunt was the same sound as the first part of the most commonly used word in Cantonese, *hiya*. *Hiya* was used for everything from 'yes' to 'I know what you mean'. But *hi* said in a really high tone was cunt. The day John was in his boxers marching around our 700-square-foot apartment with the phone to his ear. He kept getting these cold calls in Cantonese from banks for credit cards. They talked right through him even when he said *ngoi m' sic guandongwa* (sorry, my Cantonese is not good). Then he tried saying things like *choi sum* or *dung lai cha* (vegetables and cold milk tea) but they still talked right over him. So instead of saying *hiya*, *hiya*, *hiya* he shouts *hi*, then *hi* again, and again, as if he was a foreigner really trying hard to say *hiya*. It nearly always worked. They hung up fast enough.

Sometimes I feel a strange feeling creep up inside. I get angry and I use his own words at him. Fecking langer. Leaves me behind. Gets himself infected and holes up in quarantine and then talks about fecking off to his parents. He must have the world record for quarantine. What's he doing in there anyway? Does he expect me to believe him? I've been having strange dreams. I never remember dreams but this time they are vivid, and they feel real.

I met Connie for a facemask coffee. She was someone in my quarantine bubble. She had her COACH facemask holder in front of her on the table. The restaurants had installed these flimsy plastic barriers between tables. It only reached up to our eyes and every time someone passed by, it shook like a leaf in the breeze.

- 'Sue, you should forget about John. He was always such a loner anyways. Couldn't make it at home and then he found Hong Kong was no different. He'll never be happy anywhere. And now, he's still in quarantine and then you say he's going back to his parents!'
- 'Well, it won't be for long he says. But I do feel so used sometimes.'
- 'It's your chance to find someone else. Maybe go home. Whatever happened to Yuk-ling? Why are you still attracted to western guys? It's a hang up. All the drink and the fatty food. They look much worse when they get into their forties and they might be longer, but they never last as long. Believe me. Aren't I right?'
- 'You're asking the wrong woman!'
- 'Well, just so you know, I had a Chinese guy who was into Zen Buddhism. Best sex I've ever had. He wouldn't hear of condoms, but I was on the pill anyway. All night we were

doing it. Pity he joined the monastery. Still write to him though and we talk about it. May get him to leave yet.'

- 'Well, I might just get on to Yuk-ling. But last I heard he was heading for Europe.'

We laughed.

As I said it, I remembered the time John and I came home from Nathan Road. Got the taxi to Kwun Tong. He was staying in one of those serviced apartments. His toilet never flushed properly. Put me right off the nice breakfast he made for me the next morning. Bits of his shit swirling around beneath me and his croissants steaming on the kitchen table just outside. The smell of coffee. But the night before, when we'd got home, we made straight for the bedroom. We both knew what we needed.

Now that we haven't touched for months those early days of love-making come back more vividly than ever. We're in the standard-sized bedroom and he's going at me with his grim stare like it's a sex assignment. Like some sex judge is grading. He's staring at me like he's got to get through it all the right way. Half way through I say let's change position, so I get up on all fours on the bed and it's easier for him. Simple physics, I'm thinking. He's red-faced and trying to act like he does it all the time. But he's trying to find a way in and he's fingering me all wrong and he's getting frustrated, so I take his sex in my hand and guide it in and I'm barely wet so it's sore and he rocks like he's using a pneumatic drill, so I shout 'aiya aiya' and he gets the point, so he's slower now but, in all his excitement, he's done after three or four thrusts and I'm only getting started and he stays above me like a dripping dog, his hair sheeny like Siu Fei after the shower and he's hanging the sagging condom off him like it's milk of the gods and I'm itching to finish, so I only let him rub me but it's like he's trying to find an airhole in a leaking tyre and it's getting sticky so I roll over and his belly is hanging down and it's a right turn off, so I turn away and try to hold the moment in my head. Always the way, but I knew

I had him hooked. Those western women with their confident foreplay followed by them sitting on his face would never do it that way. Too high and mighty they are. Too much above it all they are. Gravity is gravity. Don't we all know they like it no other way? Like the dogs do it or like the cows do it every day around us in our village in Sai Kung. Laughing at them after our coffee. Seeing the bulls clambering all over the beige fleshy flanks of the brown, sleepy-eyed cows. I was smiling now to myself. I know it. And I know Connie will be able to see it and what she'll say. Connie could see the smile through the mask and the eyes confirmed it. The eyes told her and she knew what they meant.

-   'Look Sue, I know you like him, but he's gone. You don't really believe all that stuff about him needing to help his parents?'

John

I'm giving up the writing. Who am I fooling? This state of emergency calls for something more from me. I've decided to end the charade. Writing is too needy. It demands some kind of recognition or appeal for notoriety. Now there are too many that are seriously needy. From here on, there's to be no more writing. From here on there is no more pretence.

I called my mother again and for a moment, it was like I was there. I could see it all clearly: My father had put a cup of Barry's Tea with milk and no sugar down in front of me together with a slice of white toast slathered with apricot jam. I was staring out at the back garden watching the cats waiting for food on the windowsill. One of them, the mother, was up on her hind legs pawing the window panes. Her underside on full display. She was doing it for her young, I told myself.

My mother was waking up and raising the bed so she could have her breakfast. My father was going in for his wash. He did the strip wash. Yes, I was back there. I needed to imagine what it was like. To focus on the care I hadn't given for so long. The two of them so vulnerable and no one on the ground near them.

I'd give up the Coffee Dock too if it wasn't for that councillor. It's my last point of contact with people in here. Who knows when we're getting out. Something about her intrigues me. The care with which she folded that mask away. The way she drinks that bad coffee. Watching her, you'd never think we were in the middle of a pandemic. But there was too much of a crowd in there now. In quarantine, I always imagined it would be quieter. One does not want to get re-infected in quarantine. I need a quarantine from the quarantine. Somewhere I can go so that I feel my life is not defined by the disease.

I have a colleague in here who tells me he hates stories. 'I hate stories. I hate them all.' I don't know how we can even talk since I feel I'm made of stories. I spend all my time trying to make them up, remember them, or understand them. But like jilted lovers, the quarantine has brought us together. We meet up and talk over a coffee and a lemon tea in the Dock. He tells me about how the day his father died he was giving a talk at an academic conference. I don't like to remind him how many times he has gone back to this story each time we've met. Understandably, sometimes he tears up when he tells the story. I ask myself if he keeps going back to it because he tells himself he hates stories. He never recognizes one when it comes along, so he ends up repeating it. I try to stop myself treating anything he tells me like a story but then I get the feeling he's almost urging me to tell him what it all means. Maybe he's denying himself the resolution only story can bring. I say something.

- 'That must have been so tough.'

His eyes agree and look like they want to tell me more. But instead he talks about work again. The moment is gone.

- 'I have a paper to get done but I just don't have the head for it.'

Sometimes he visibly grimaces when we're talking as if he's telling himself to shut up. I tell myself he's trying to stop himself telling stories. It's like he's forever giving me good beginnings for stories he never wants to finish.

We're living in a no-touch society. Socially distancing and self-isolating are no good for touch. I recall now with fondness the touch of my wife, the tracing of a finger along her skin, a casual massage of a tight shoulder. I remember sex and touching with a sense of nostalgia. It's not even the sex but just the holding of hands and the embracing. It's all gone now. A touchless world. It's funny how the memories of a sense blossom in its absence. I'm remembering moments and sensations that were previously nothing to me. How we used to shake hands with departing friends. The last time I shook my Uncle Michael's hand. His workman's clasp reduced to a gentle caress from illness. Those long kisses with old girlfriends. It was intoxicating, time-bending. I don't think young people find it the same way today if even they could with no one touching. They're being pushed more and more online when their bodies are crying out for touch.

Truth be told, sometimes I like quarantine. It's a break from what I recall now of my sick boy. Oh, but how I miss him! It was never all plain sailing. The life of a father. My daily routine was so regular. But what I wouldn't give to get it back. Babies only know touch. They survive on it. The wailing when they're put down, away from the press of warm bodies and warm hands.

You wake up to his crying and see him standing over you in the cot. You switch the fan on first thing, the one you bought with the gold rotor cap. You rock him for thirty minutes and he cries and arches his body. He fights with all his might against you. He pulls out your chest hairs. He kicks into your abdomen. You try and feed him, but he will not take the milk. He starts to cry and wail non-stop for ten minutes, then twenty minutes. You give him a dummy, but he spits it out. He prefers to wail and cry. You try to feed him again. He takes the nipple in his mouth but won't suck. You hold it in his mouth for five minutes, ten minutes, but still no sucking. You put him on the play mat and he vomits all over the clothes you had just changed him into. You put him on the changing table and change his nappy and his clothes. You put him back in the Combi high chair. He begins to wail and cry again and pushes with all his might against the straps. Again you try to feed him but he will not take the nipple. You know he is tired, but he won't sleep. You rock him again standing in front of the fan. You sing all the lines of all the songs you think will send him to sleep. He arches his back and wrestles with all his might against you. Your back is aching, and your biceps are straining. You rest him against your chest as you rock him. Still he wrestles and arches his back. Now a good two hours have gone. You have put off work deadlines. You will have to wash and bathe him soon and then feed him. Then the cycles will begin again. It is 3 p.m. and there are four or five hours to go before he sleeps. You have five days of this every week. The helper, Mandy, comes for six hours a day twice a week. Tuesdays and Thursdays. It is Friday. All your days are like this. Previously, you had time to yourself. Now, you can't think too much about the time you have lost or the time you will lose long into the future. You simply couldn't conceive of what it would feel like when you were trying for so long and then going through all the expensive courses of treatment. You wonder with amazement how your mother brought up five young children in the '70s and '80s on her own most of the time. You feel guilty when you sit at the table reading and he is wailing or crying. You are neglecting him. He will remember it. The sensation of being neglected will leave an imprint on his character. He will become sullen and inward-looking. He will become shy. He will shun friendly advances. Will he retreat into himself? You run to stand over him as he plays on the mat. You jump around in front of him and smile and make silly faces. He doesn't smile back. He looks back at you as if to say, 'what are you doing?' He sees through you. He sees you're not being authentic. Be authentic with him. Don't introduce him to falsity. What does the good book say about falsity. You've forgotten. You never knew what it said. You and your wife are to blame. You build narratives out of the slightest frown, the subtlest of grimaces or smiles. What else can you build around him but future narratives? He has no past. His present is a blur of need. Yes, there are cycles. You know them well. But he stumbles from stage to stage of a cycle like a drunk man stumbling from bar to bar. He's wailing again from the high chair. He has finished sucking his hands. You give him the dummy, but he spits it out. You give him the nipple. He begins to suck. You can see the bubbles rising up through the milk. You feel elated. You begin to relax back into your contemplation of the next ten minutes. You can live on autopilot for ten minutes. But then a frown comes on his face and he turns red. He is straining and you hear the low guttural sound of his straining. Your suspicions are confirmed as the stench rises from his body. You had just strapped him in to the high chair. You unstrap him again. His belly is pushed right up against the clasp of the straps, so it is difficult to untie him. You carry him to the changing table. There is no cup of water for the cotton pads. Where are the baby wipes? You cannot leave him alone on the changing table. You must carry him around with you as you search for each item. His face is red now from wailing. You see the Tupperware container of cotton wool buds, cotton pads and cotton q-tips. You grab it and bring it back to the changing table. Change of clothes. You need a change of clothes. You lift him again and carry him into the bedroom. You carry him in one arm as you try the drawer. He arches his back and it is hard to hold him. You can feel the biceps of your right arm straining like never before. You know you have done it some damage. You find an outfit for him in the drawer. You bring him back to the changing table. You unbutton the one-piece and high up above the waistband of the nappy you see stains of shit. You unseal the nappy. A spray of hot liquid hits you in the face as you bend down to inspect the mess in his nappy. He is urinating on you. You push the dirty nappy back against his penis. The soiled nappy has stained his back up high. The urine mixed with shit runs down his legs. You start with the baby wipes and work them back and forth along his lower abdomen and soiled body. After about five baby wipes you switch to cotton pads soaked in water. The shit comes away slowly. The grooves in between the legs and the testicles are lined with yellow, creamy shit. You spread his legs and wipe every crevice.

After a bundle of baby wipes, nappy and cotton pads is fully soiled you wash him again with wet cotton pads. He is smiling and playing with his hands. You imagine what he will be like with his partners. When the shit has changed. When he is more in control of his body. He wouldn't get very far if he didn't move on from this. It's a long road ahead, son. I'm with you all the way. You know he will rarely acknowledge this work you've done for him. As you never acknowledged this work your own father and mother did for you. There are things we can't say. You bend down to search for a nappy and he pushes himself backwards on the changing table, almost pushing himself off. It is a four-foot drop. You must watch him. You put on a new nappy and a clean top from the drawer. You take a bib with you as you carry him back from the changing table to the Combi. He vomits over your shirt and all over his new top as you carry him back. You needed to put the bib on quicker. You are learning. You tell yourself you are learning. You carry him back to the changing table. You need a new top. You carry him with you to the chest of drawers in the bedroom. You rummage around for a new top. There is nothing left. You find a shorts and t-shirt. You carry him back to the changing table. Getting his wriggling arms out of the vomit-sodden one-piece is a struggle. Who made these things? When you pull the tight neck of the top over his head it gets stuck. You accidentally scratch the top of his head with your fingernail. He is wailing now. He is almost screaming. You take him up close to your chest and try to comfort him. He arches his back. He vomits again over the new top on the changing table. He is red-faced again. You hear that intake of breath. That moment of silence before the ear-shattering wail. You must calm him down before you do anything else. The deadlines for work flash briefly across your mind. You don't give them a second thought. He is wriggling again with all his might. You see yourself in that struggling. You see it as your strength, what you have prided yourself on. Your ability to stand your ground. Some people, including your mother, have called it stubbornness. You realize you are fighting against yourself. You know its strength, but now it is directed against you. Taste of your own medicine. You smirk at the justice of it all. You change him. You carry him back into the front room and put him gently down on the play mat. You can see the droplets of fine tears on his tiny eye lashes. It will be your image for innocence. He is smiling now as you dance to pretend music. You recognize in his smile his desire to be good. You start to wonder if he is smiling because he wants you to think him a good boy. Is this the beginning of him learning to be eager to please? You must not encourage it. Where did it ever get you? You want him to draw from something else. You want him to have some of your wife's playfulness, her ability to react to things without overthinking. That's what he needs. None of the brooding. Play will do it. Play with him. You lie down beside him on the play mat. What kind of play? You reach for a Miffy book. No, not yet. Don't give him the book yet. Give him some more time without the rule of the book and the page and the written word. The first prison house is the prison house of language. Imagine what we might become without the printed word? My book is closed, I read no more. I watch the fire dance on the floor. Who was that again? Ah, yes. No one he should listen to yet. But then you wonder if his growing brain needs language and the printed word as early as possible. Get that brain working. That's the mantra. Get the brain working fast. Don't give them too much undirected and self-directed time. Get his routines working. Get the sleep time down. What was it your neighbour called himself? A boot-camp instructor. Yes, in the Singaporean army. Get everything down fast and have them remember it. Self-directed learning. That buzz word in education that only allows the students to think they're calling the shots. All worked out long before they get to the self-access centre. Self-access, my arse. He's smiling again. Dance. Sing to him. Don't leave him for too long in his own company. Don't leave him for hours staring into the electric fan. The electric fan with the gold rotor. Staring into the gold-capped rotor of the rotating fan he shall find his way. Learn to spin on his own axis. Engage in repetitive motion. Get the routines down. Even the fan seems to tell him that. But then you never know. He's seeing everything his own way. What dreams might he get looking at it? He's wailing again. It's nearly 5. One more feed at 5.30, then he'll sleep again after seven. You lift him up, off the play mat. You rock him gently in your arms and sing him the 'Cliffs of Duneen'. It has become his song. You started singing it in the early days out of desperation. The repetitive singing of it put him to sleep. Now you sing it again. His eyelids are heavy. He is staring into the gold rotor. The fan speed is on three. You hope it will not be too strong for him. Like the harsh winds that lie ahead. You can't conceive of the pain they will cause him. A boy you helped bring into the world. This care has brought you closer to him and you've only done it now for four months. Years of care lie ahead. How can you ever let him face those winds alone? This is the training. Your training. You are being taught to bond with him. You will bond with him like no other. No one else has taken up so much of your time. No one else has ever allowed you to see them so vulnerable for so long. No one else will teach you to care so much for so long.

After a few months of looking after him, you remember how you returned to the day job because you needed more money. These memories cause you such pain now. In quarantine, you ask yourself if you will see so many of the familiar things again. You feel a sense of guilt for the little things you have done. You recall coming home one evening about six in the evening. You see the baby in the cot in the living room and a cry rises up somewhere inside of you. He is crying and wants to sleep. You know the routine. This is your terrain. You take him up. He arches his back. You rock him, swing him about gently, sing to him. You know the ropes. You're holding him for twenty minutes, twenty-five minutes. Still he shrieks and wails and pushes out against you with all his strength. You are still wound up from work you tell yourself.

Something a colleague said. The way the office staff greeted you. He is digging in. His wailing is rising in pitch. Sue is having a moment of glorious me-time at the table. 'Can you help me and get the feckin' dummy?' You want to take it back as soon as it's said. Sue takes the baby from you. The crying stops instantly and he's drinking the milk you couldn't feed him. You will never be the one. You will never have that connection. The connection a mother has with a child. You are like a shadow or a stone. You rub up against him. He cries in your bony arms. You will never know what it's like to have the assurance of connection. All your life you will seek it out and only ever see it given without thought to mothers. You feel it like a pain, but you know you will get through it. The deadlines flash across your mind again. You are ready for them. You will take them on.

You recall the time you all went to Cork. How your parents realized it was all too much for them early on in your visit. You were the last man standing. Sam had them all down with injuries—Sue and both your parents. Sue had her trigger finger, thumb and wrist in a sling from the strain of lifting him. Your father, who's eighty-three, put his back out carrying him. He lay on the flat of his back for three days. His back is still painful. Your mother's knees are always so sore. She can't walk very well. Sam kept kicking his legs into her bad left knee as he lay on her lap, again and again, as he refused to take the milk. It was vicious. She was on painkillers and kept rubbing Deep Heat in all day. She couldn't go near Sam in the end what with all the Deep Heat. You were the last one standing. The last one to be able to go near him. And now the load is affecting you. On two or three occasions you've noticed a worsening of your hip pain from your knee injury. As you rock him, each time he won't sleep, you can almost feel the ball and socket joint grinding away. You think of the years he is taking off your ability to walk unaided. You love him. Your baby boy. Your miracle.

Phoebe

I read a report today from a writer, aged sixty-five, in Wuhan. She describes the bodies zipped up in bags and trucked to the crematorium. She writes of the old people waiting for long hours in the cold and rain to see if there is a bed. Queueing hour after hour beside the infected in the pouring rain, only to be told there is no bed. Some try to reserve a bed before they come only to be told it's gone when they arrive.

Living as a single woman, all I had was Tinder, the gym and the cinema. They're all off limits now. My sister is temping in London and she has to commute for three hours a day on packed tubes. I too get nostalgic about simple things we might never do the same way again. Eating hot pot together.

But I'm leaving the 24-hour Quarantine Coffee Dock today. Told John it was the last time I'd be there. Didn't know if he'd show up. But we had our plan. Then I saw him, when I was leaving. We walked out keeping two metres apart. I was walking ahead. I knew where I was going and what we would do. It had been too long. We both needed to do this. He had a high temperature again, but this wasn't an issue for us, the long-tails of quarantine. They had given me new sheets for my bed. The good thing about quarantine is I didn't have to share a room with my mother. I could feel his eyes on me. I felt a warmth and an excitement inside like burning, a burning that wasn't fever. It had been so long. I could almost taste it. I longed again for the taste of touch. It would not be long now. I had already worked it out. We would have enough time. Even if they saw something, it would take them a long time to come to my room. Possibly hours. I had finally worked out how to live. I was going to give myself up to infection.

John

I sit alone here, and the skies and roads are quiet. The spike has continued. It is no longer a spike. More like an endless climb. The skies are clear for the first time since I moved here, and the air feels unpolluted. Hong Kong has never looked so good. How often pilots would welcome us with, 'It's a bright morning in Hong Kong with the familiar yellow haze.' Hong Kong was waking up to see itself like it had never seen itself. Nature is taking a deep breath. Not so for us.

As I sit here on the balcony of my small room in quarantine, I stare for possibly the last time at the cloud above Mount Stenhouse. I have become more aware than ever before of our distance from nature. Even though they are telling us that the virus has come from nature, it is only killing humans. Birds are not falling from the sky, our seas and rivers are not full of dead fish, and our pets are generally going about their business. The micro-droplets are only infecting and killing humans. We have found a way to distinguish ourselves from nature, something we have been so eager to prove. But it is only in our dying that we recall our dependence on nature. All around us, nature blossoms and blooms in the warmth of another bountiful spring. Nature stares on us from the heights of Tai Mo Shan and from the depths of the seas around Lamma and it seems to be saying, 'Take care, we have done all we can to nurture you, to feed you, to sustain you, but now you are on your own. You have turned us against you, and it is part of what we are that is doing this, but we no longer understand it. It has changed beyond our recognition.'

Phoebe and I are meeting tomorrow. We will celebrate our decision to leave the quarantine coffee behind us. We've decided to break the rules. To step inside the two-metre safe zones that surround us and keep us apart. Feeling excited. You need something to motivate you, to keep you going. Even in quarantine, when you're a long-tail and there seems no way out.

But I'm getting out. And when I do, I'll leave for Ireland and my parents. I must do what I can for them. They're both vulnerable and in their mid-eighties. Sue said she's leaving the flat if I go. I understand. How much more waiting can she take? She will stay with her mother. I've told her I have to do it.

Pangolin

It was hard going. I had been burrowing through undergrowth for hours now without looking up. My snout was cut by the brambles and twigs. I didn't know how much longer I could run. The touch of those hands around me still sent shivers through me. I hadn't heard the whine of a single pangolin. The incline had continued for many hours. The air felt thinner. I will stop soon and feed. I can see there were ant hills here. Pretty soon I will feel my old self. My young are gone now. Three years I reared them. Lost, back in the valleys, to the poachers. I will remain solitary now and only venture out in the dead of night. It was the way we used to be. The way we were meant to be until we started getting sick. Then everyone feasted at all hours and even in groups. We lost track of ourselves. I will rebuild in this mountain. I'll live away from fear and, who knows, maybe the rains and the change of season will bring me a second chance.

III

Hong Kong/Cork
June–July, 2020

John

When I got out of quarantine, I went back to see if I could help my parents in Ireland. It was a tough decision. Taking the risk of bringing it back, only so I could be in the same town as them. 400 metres away. A three-minute walk. Self-isolating in an empty house on the other side of the road. Only to be there to deliver their shopping and medicine to them when they needed it. It all seemed to make such sense until I mentioned it to friends over there.

I came back on the last flight to leave Hong Kong. As soon as I left quarantine. Ordered away from Phoebe and the rest of the diseased. I knew what I had to do. I would leave my wife and my sick boy until I knew my parents were safe. My Penelope and Telemachus. He has his work, I mine. But I'm no Ulysses. The only demons and monsters I fought off in quarantine were of my own making. But I knew I would return home. I always knew and I keep telling myself. Sometimes I feel I renounced something sacred in my quarantine because of this disease. In my long hours of quarantine, I started to feel the disease had infiltrated me so that the world inside no longer seemed connected to the one outside. I grew desperate. I became obsessed by the possibility of a happy death. Who was it who put it in my mind? Yes, possibly Camus and all his talk about the benign indifference of the universe. It was a kind of offering. I was intent on offering myself up to a happy death so I would beat the virus. The person who acted then was indeed a stranger. A stranger to me now. I cannot correlate the two. I did what I did as a challenge to the virus. It was an affront to infection. It was a revolt, not an aberration. But no one will ever see it like that. They will not even see me. I don't know if they will ever see me again.

I see them through the glass darkly. My own parents. It's worse being here. Two metres away and it feels worse than being thousands of miles away. My nightly calls from quarantine in Hong Kong brought them nearer than they feel now. Seeing them physically without being able to go near them, I feel our separation more intensely. But I must do what I can. Every day I leave shopping bags inside the porch, close the porch door behind me, and retreat half way down the driveway. I turn back to face the door. I must be six feet away. My father opens the door and looks at me. He casts his eyes down, his shoulders sink a little and I can see his eyes tear up. I wasn't prepared for this. I should never have come back. When they let me out, I wanted to act. I didn't want to think about what I was going to do for too long. I booked the last flight back to see them.

Friends here were furious when I told them I was coming back. 'Stay away!' they said. 'Stay away, for the love of our country. Jesus!' These were the words of my best friends. The 'our country' seemed to exclude me. I didn't feel like it invited me in. The 'Jesus' seemed almost shocking for a couple that I knew were so anti-religious. I knew it was meant as a kind of gasp of shock at the end of their plea, a crowning moment of appeal. Seeing the word 'Jesus' made me realize how insistent they were. Surely they acknowledged they were appealing to a higher power of some kind? How could they ask me to follow reason and logic, and then use the word 'Jesus'? Of course, they might simply be swearing. 'Jesus!' as in, 'you're not serious.' 'Jesus!' as in, 'what the feck are ye playing at?' But it still hurt. For this was all we were left with now. Texts, missed calls, the odd video chat. Each one carried so much weight. Each text was like a short story. I told myself I was being over-sensitive. I should get a grip. All the same I couldn't help feeling I would lose a friend if I returned. In my quiet moments, I would go over the words. The few words from them on the screen made me sound dishonest, like a schemer, like someone who used every means at his disposal to dodge the truth. Cherry-picking he called it. He said I couldn't see how I was acting out of fear. When I told him I was acting out of love, there was silence. Nothing but silence. Or the absence of words. Their words presumed I was bent on deception. I was wilfully ignorant of the truth. I was a type. 'There you go again twisting the facts.' 'FUUUCK, you just don't get it. You are just cherry-picking.' Never once did they respond to me as if there was any truth in me acting out of what I called love for my family. I liked nothing about the portrait painted of me by their words. It was detestable. It was nothing like the self-portrait I had constructed inside according to which I was someone who was a little worldly wise, reflective and capable of care. Instead I was being painted as this low-grade deceiver.

As my father took up the plastic bags and looked at me with a kind of sadness I had never seen from him, I realized that being here was hurting them more than if I had stayed away. At least halfway across the world, they could understand not having me to hug or talk to in person. Here it was too strange, too sad.

John

I sit alone in this unfurnished house. All I have is electricity, gas and water. No internet and no TV. My sister said she couldn't survive here. Not because of the virus but because there was no internet. I had brought my yoga mat from Hong Kong. I sleep in the centre of the large empty room that was to be our living room. Living room. Even the names of rooms take on new meaning now. There should be a dying room in every villa in northern Italy. A room to remember the dead.

There are no streetlights outside my window. It's pitch black from nightfall until I see the first glimmer of light from the sun rising, out over the Lee Valley and down towards the harbour. The windows and roofs of the old Georgian houses along Gardiner's Hill and Ballyhooly Road catch the first rays and tell me another day is dawning. I don't know any of my neighbours. My house is in a small terrace of seven houses, each one smaller than the next. I'm in house number two. I bought the house during the downturn. It was riddled with damp. Knocked a wall away due to the rising damp. 'Capillary damp' the builder called it. Tried to do as much myself as I could. Watched all the YouTube videos on plastering and tiling and even on support work for ceilings. Demolished an old seventies-style external chimney feature that rose two floors, brick by brick. Left the electrics and gas to local tradesmen. The whole job took about three years. Had a carpenter put in a built-in wardrobe for Sue in the bedroom. A gift for her to help her feel better about the move. I had the old water tank and hot press moved out of an ugly cupboard in the box room. All so my sick boy would have a cupboard of his own. Put in a cupboard and pull-out desk myself and sanded the corners until they shone like marble. I was going to open the large window over the stairs to the flat roof of the bathroom and put a roof garden out there. Maybe even a chair and tables if the roof was supported. We had plans. They came unbidden like thought itself. Thought presumes a future of some kind. I'm hungry; I must eat. I'm thirsty; I must drink. I work; I must see the fruits of my labour. I never really questioned making plans. Now there are no plans. Or different plans. Plans that make no sense to the old me, the me working on this house. Plans for how I will refrigerate my parents' food after bulk-buying? Plans for how I keep one or two weeks ahead of the food needs of my parents? Plans for how I will order enough for them to prevent them from ever having to go out? I know how my eighty-three-year-old father likes to walk to the corner shop. It's like getting up for him. He dresses up for it. Shirt and tie and his best shoes and trousers. His good brown shoes from the hall. How can I ever buy enough or do enough to keep him inside? They need to stay inside. He's stubborn. Like his mother. He won't learn something unless he has to. I try to imagine how he thinks. *What's the rush? I know what I know and what I need to know. Didn't I teach myself remote control over the years. I know my limits. I know what I can do and what I must do.* I knew that going to the shop was in the must do category for Dad. It is a performance perfected over many years. When my mother was well and she did the shopping or we went down for orders, Dad didn't like going to the shop. There was the embarrassment of it all. Now, in a new house and with those shops long gone, some of their buildings demolished, and some of the former shop-owners dead, Dad goes to the shop more often. Since he needed to care for my mother, he has also gone most days to the local shop. But it would have to be a certain kind of shop for my dad to enjoy frequenting it. One he could relate to. If the people of the shop were from down the country—West Cork being the ideal—then it became interesting. If the shop had a solid history of people working in a way that clearly went beyond commercial interests and spoke to service to the community, then even better. If there was a family tradition attached to the shop, better still. And if you could hear in the local papers about an older member of that family passing away, an older member who had perhaps opened the shop a generation or two ago in the '50s and passed it down to the daughter and then the granddaughter and you could go to the removal and walk to the top of the Removal Hall like everyone else or later that week to the top of the church at the funeral in the same parish and pay your respects to the current shopkeeper—the granddaughter—and be recognized, then better again. That was the kind of shop you would like to shop in. And, if the current owner of the shop was a woman about sixty, with a name like Regina, a name you knew could also be pronounced in your schoolboy Latin, the way Regina was in those prayers to Mary Queen of Souls that you chanted aloud in the boarding school in Killarney in the '50s, then you found you could go to that shop. And you would wear your shirt and tie and trousers and good brown shoes and best jacket when you did.

I somehow had to stop this habit of my father. It was no easy task. There was an unquestioned almost devotional attention to care and to Mum in his actions sometimes that went beyond any tint of commercialism. Since our conversations were so brief now, my father never being entirely comfortable with virtual chats, I imagined him in front of me. How would we ever talk about it otherwise? Hadn't you always striven to keep free of this, of what to do with money, of how the earnings went on the big shop each fortnight? Preferring not to pay the bills yourself? Never happy withdrawing it? Happy to see others do it. And when you finally had some money to put into the top pocket of your jacket, the one you could zip up, you gave it out freely and with grace. Every beggar, every taxi man, got their tips. Every man who collected shopping trolleys got tips. You knew the names of the men down on their luck in the homeless shelter and they got a fiver when you had it. The insistent Romanian women who followed you over Brian Boru Bridge or Patrick's Street with their babies in their arms always came away smiling. Money was a blessing. It was grace itself. It was about more than monetary value. It bestowed its grace on whoever was needy and this filled your heart. And if you hadn't the money, you preferred to stay inside and wait until you had an opportunity again to share the good grace.

Lying alone in the dark, empty house, I realized I couldn't keep you inside during the pandemic. The freedom to walk outside is life itself to you and you see it as part of this life of grace-giving. Not to be able to walk out was unthinkable and not worth conceiving of as a way of life.

There's something purifying about this quarantine. My day is filled with a sense of enduring urgency. And yet I can settle to nothing. I climb the stairs to the attic room until I am exhausted. The old house has thirty-two steps inside and a garden out the front. Sam was meant to be playing in it. Sue was going to have her hydrangea over in the corner. We were going to bring the old plant back to life. Sometimes at twilight, I imagine I see them out there, playing together in the long, unkempt grass.

I never knew walking a house could wear you out. Up and down I go until the stairs creak and the old bannister starts to give a little. When I'm spent, I lie down on the floor of the living room, my back resting against the stairs. I see the quiet waters of the Lee roll out to the harbour. The fields stretch off to the countryside on the horizon. This city doth like a garment wear the beauty of the morning. How the great heart is lying still. Wordsworth wasn't it? But I can make no appeal to Triton or Proteus. The virus is invisible. We too must learn in our own time how the world is too much with us and we must rid ourselves of it. I must find ways to stay away from people while keeping myself and those I love alive. Even offers to help out of goodwill can kill. This city below me looks so placid, so calm. The virus is invisible and yet we know it's there. How many times have I heard them call depression and loneliness silent killers? Well now we have a new silent killer, and it wants to make us all as lonely as possible and it cares nothing for depression.

I descend the stairs slowly in the empty house. The house was built in the 1840s, just before the Great Famine. The biggest killer ever of people in this country. Caused too by disease, by a blight, but one that only hit the potato, the people's staple. Today, they are not so reliant on a single food source. Only the virus is feasting on its human staple.

What did you do during the war? Everyone says this is like a war. Well, what did you do during the war then? I sometimes aim the question at myself as I lie awake in the dark, empty house. It's what they used to ask James Joyce. He'd taken his family with him and hid away from the carnage in Trieste, in Pula, in Paris, in Zurich. Always running. Always crossing borders. With wars raging over the hills, he wrote of soap and potted meat, of kidney and gambling on throwaways. Never a word on the war. He kept his head down. I can't stop thinking about it, this war. At least I can try too and keep my head down for a part of each day and I'll take inspiration from wherever I can. He locked himself away in a small chalet on the shores of Lake Garda to begin his work of isolation. He would never see his parents again. Never see his homeland. At least I could come back.

I am completely alone. In some ways it is purifying. It is fitting that this house too is empty and devoid of any ornament or object except my bag and this yoga mat. My own parents look at me aghast as if to say, 'Why have you come?' 'What can you do for us other than remind us of what we have lost?' 'What about your wife and son? Why are you not with them?' There is no way back now. They have closed the airports and the borders. No one is allowed out.

John

As I lie here in the dark, in the empty room, I'm visited by flashbacks of what now feels like a former life. Some kind of withdrawal symptom perhaps. That Bilbao summer on the beach. Tracking back off the Camino de Santiago de Compostela pilgrimage trail for some sun and sand at Bilbao. The close-knit tents of trance music. The crowds of bronzed, young people on the beach. Hanging out of each other's tents. Sprawling topless, both the men and the women. Joseph and I trying to sunbathe. The sand burning the soles of my feet. I make a break for the sea, running in my white flesh. My eyes focused on the blue sea, ignoring through pain the women bathing topless with their skin like oak, sunning themselves all around me. My white, hairy body scampering across the sands as if I'd been unearthed from years of lying asleep under the sands. I look back at Joseph stripping off, a pale, sun-starved stalk in a field of gold. Running for the cover of the sea-blue sea, shimmering now like some crystal balm to heal the burning skin of my burning feet. I dive before I know where the water is. I need to get out of the heat burning my head and neck and off the sand burning the soles of my feet. But the water is too shallow. When I land—even though I had never truly left the ground—I'm doggy-paddling like some overgrown child, my toes hitting shell and rock, my hands scraping shingle. Spurts of water escaping from me like jets. I'm struggling to get all my body under the water. Then the calming seas surround me like soothing balm. I see shimmering light above me as I swim further out underwater. Dark shapes loom above me breaking the light. I surface and all around me are young Spanish women splashing their naked torsos with saltwater, blinding sunshine illuminating their skin. I emerge in their midst like some grizzled squid and they respectfully make way. My Nausicaa moment. My Bilbao Nausicaa moment. Their beauty confronts me, and I realize I haven't been staring. I was momentarily living among them. I was one of them. A sea-nymph sporting among them in the life-gorged, self-forgetful sands of time. But then my feet hit the ground and I'm back with myself. I'm telling myself not to stare. I retreat back up the sands to my rucksack, scuttling back on the scorching sands with my temples burning with passion and sunburn and this rush of humanity.

Sarah Ryan

Your coming back, your standing here in full view. So close and yet so far. It pains us to the heart's core. Only because we love you so and want the best for you. It only makes us taste all the stronger our physical isolation. Why did you leave them behind? You can be such a foolish son sometimes. Couldn't you read between the lines? I never could tell you outright not to come back. Tell you what was best for you. I could never hurt you like that. But surely you must have known. You were always such a clever boy but a romantic too, like your father. Your head in the books. Cut off from what was going on around you. Your father brought us back here from London and it wasn't an easy thing to do. It took all his passion and willpower. And he is a stubborn man too and you are like your father. You, inside my belly. You, growing inside me through the biggest and most traumatic move of my life. And did I ever tell you I never was sure all through it, all through the move. Four months pregnant with you and us preparing to leave my homeland forever, to go and live with a strange people, a people I did not know and who would never accept me into their hearts. Those were the times we were living in in the '70s. There were bombs going off and people were being imprisoned unjustly. There was such distrust between the two countries. How could I ever expect them to welcome us with open arms. But I was unprepared too for the slights and the coldness. I felt so isolated sometimes. Leaving behind a life in London that seemed so modern and bright next to what we arrived into. I know they call *this* self-isolation and lockdown today. But if you only knew, my son. The long silent years of isolation. This is child's play. Half my life among a people I could only be on guard with, a people with a great capacity for ridicule and aggression despite all their talk and promises. So, I have had my preparation for this time of lockdown you might say. At least now there is no pretence. At least now there is no performance. I no longer need to worry about performing my compliance to win their favour. To be mindful of their ways and their spites. My performance had been too good over the years. I lost the trace of who I was. I lost the trace of that working woman, working in the City of London, in the banks and the commercial districts. Now, I feel I can find that person again. No one needs to step foot inside here again unless they truly want to. Only my sons and my daughter and all of us together when the virus is long gone. I never again have to worry about their acceptance as me and Tim have the time now to spend our days together. Our love has withstood all. Now at last I am able to give time to us and to be with your father. Even you, my own son, can be forgetful. Sometimes you can't read the signs. Couldn't you see how it would be? Give us this time. These days our daily bread. At last we will have the days to be able to spend real time together alone. Real time together without the call to be a mother. It is all they can see me as. I played my part too well. One role leads to another. But I am reclaiming myself. I am finding parts of me that go a long way back. Back to a London, long before the virus, long before the days my father carried me in his arms into the bomb shelters with Hitler's doodlebugs shaking the buildings on our street.

It's the old Irish deceit. I've had it all my life. The problem is their writers are all poets and drunks. The ones that really mattered to the rest of the world all had to leave or were called Anglo-Irish, people they could never accept even though they were from the same stock. If you went back far enough, we were all from the same stock. All the rest who made any name for themselves had to move to my hometown, London town. Leaving Ireland in order to write about it. Didn't he ever understand? They could never stick the place, but still they keep making their readers feel they must return. The last laugh is with them. Yeats couldn't stick his small cabin built here of clay and wattles. He would only go and build himself a castle as far away from the real Irish as he could get and then leave it forever after only a few summers living there. The damp walls nearly killed him. And then you, John, going on about the damp in the walls in your new place and me thinking you've only gone and found your own Yeats's castle in Dillons Cross! That was the reality of it. Didn't I try to keep telling you? And you, with your own wife and child in quarantine, out there, in China. Oh, what were you thinking?

John

I'm sitting in self-isolation in the damp house in the dark. I don't want the electric light on. I want to be aware of day passing into night outside. I can hear the odd car passing and the occasional tread of footsteps on the pavements outside. I imagine stories for each stranger who passes. Some of them might even be people I knew. I wonder if they would feel something as they passed me unawares. Was there some kind of invisible connection that hung in the air between people at such times? Like Wi-Fi signals between people, so we got a hint of each other as we passed unawares but within range, in the dead of night? I imagine how thoughts of me might enter their minds as they pass on the other side of the wall. *Must give that langer, John, a call one day. He was always good for a laugh. Never could stick it here.*

I could see creatures flitting in and out of the streetlights that were visible from the living room window. Bats. Never did like them. I remember jogging near the Tolo Harbour across from Ma On Shan in Hong Kong. It was an inlet of the South China Sea. A forgotten inlet. Sometimes huge rusting tankers parked in the harbour for months on end. Ghost ships waiting to be bought. A kind of limbo for tankers. Good tankers went for cruise liner retrofitting. Bad tankers went to the great tanker graveyard off the coast of the Horn of Africa. I'd seen them for sale on Alibaba and E-bay. Used oil tanker. $18 million. Length 317.1m. What a steal. Could you see out the virus on one of them? Raise your family and then come back in off the high seas to join society? The sales template for the liners on the websites even had a

'Packaging and Delivery' section. Packaging Detail: Without. Delivery: Immediate. Receiver comes home from work, opens his post latch and finds a failed delivery-note inside. Report to local post office between 2–4 p.m. Receiver goes to collect. Whole town destroyed by the tanker's illegal parking. Gross tonnage: 122,447. Nationality: Malaysian. Contact: Ms Jenny Zhao. Even tankers had nationalities it seemed. I'd put in some bids in my spare time. Watched the price climb before the deadline. Started receiving strange emails of a threatening nature from the registered email address. Pulled out. Tanker most likely now on the high seas of international piracy.

I remember when I jogged by those rusting tankers in the Tolo Harbour at twilight. I was smeared in mosquito spray. Bats dipped and dived above me. Vampire bats? Bats have had a lot of bad press these days. They should have avoided hanging out with pangolins. I'd see them hovering right above me and I'd imagine them nipping my wrists and ankles silently in the clammy heat. I told myself I'd watched too many cheap horrors. It all seemed so far-fetched.

Phoebe

I can't leave quarantine. I'm finding it hard to think beyond Lamma. Now the government has banned all groups of four or more. We are on curfew after 6 p.m. Restaurants, the lifeblood of the community, have nearly all closed.

I remember his touch. It didn't cure me and for some reason I couldn't infect him. Try as I might. It just wouldn't stick. How he used to whisper it to me. Infect me. Infect me. Try. Try as hard as you can. Give me your worst. It will never stick. How right he was. Twisted together in each other's embrace on the damp sheets we dared not make a sound. The narrow mattress drenched, we drifted on the silent seas of our infected love. We didn't even have positions. We forgot all this. It was like those times long forgotten, those times experienced maybe only once in each lifetime, where everything happens without plot or plan and your two bodies are consumed and caught up together as if you have known each other like a second skin all your life. Freeing ourselves of the greatest fear, the fear of infection, made everything possible. There wasn't a thought for any other fear or doubt. I sometimes caught myself thinking in the middle of it, when I had a chance to take a breath, if I could only think like this all the time, I'd be indestructible. And not to only think like this all the time, but to act like this. But it never can be. Desperate times call out all our fears and show them up to be small injustices to ourselves and our own flourishing. Now with him gone, I only remember the sense of freedom. We overcame this virus. We rid ourselves of its power and found people we had forgotten existed. It could only last a few moments out of time, but some experiences help you withstand a lifetime. He didn't get infected again and if he did it was nothing more than sneezing and a gentle cough that he showed for it. We joked that we had found the cure, the drug cocktail, the antigens. 'Full-frontal exposure' he called it. For once I didn't mind. I liked to dress it up a bit more. We had infected ourselves with the courage to ignore the virus and it was contagious. We shared it willingly. Opened ourselves up to it fully. Exposed every part of our bodies. And we felt the rush of its infiltration and in its climax, we found ourselves like we never had before. I can only describe it as complete self-knowing—nothing at all like those solitary, self-induced mindfulness manoeuvres—but an intersubjective, intracorporeal self-knowing like no incarnation recorded. A new flesh may well have been created out of the disease, infection and joy. A new flesh somewhat divine in its imperviousness to attack and infection. Sadly, he took that flesh with him. I still retain this stagnant, low-level infection. It's never changed since I came to quarantine. And yet I'm beginning to see this low-level, steady-state infection as my saving grace.

It is almost always asymptomatic. Hovering between light symptoms and none. But always infected. I used to joke to him that I am a living vaccine. I am the vaccine and the infection in the one body, neutralizing them and sustaining them. He liked Marvel superheroes, so I used to joke to him, 'I am Vaccine. Try a small dose.' But we only had the one dose of each other, and it was far beyond what the prescription might demand. Living like this, living permanently on the edge, I feel I'm safe. As I watch quarantine subsume everything and as I watch the smoke from the crematorium chimney rising, I am thankful for my state. John recited a few lines from a poem to me—not even a few lines—because he said it reminded him of me. They were the only lines he said he could remember. An English teacher and he only had a few lines from one poem! He told me it was Beckett. I thought

Beckett only put grandmothers in trash cans. But this whole thing made Beckett look like comedy and nothing else.

> My peace is there [. . .]
> Where I may [. . .]
> [. . .] live the space of a door that opens and shuts.

I hear they have closed all the 24-hour McDonald's. Well not closed entirely but the seats are gone. Temperature checks at the door and a quota of people allowed inside at any one time. Just as well he wrote down what he could. At least there is some record of what we had. He's back in Ireland now. On a fool's errand. Will his parents ever be allowed to let him in? It's all so different since he left, I sometimes wonder if it ever happened at all. It could have been a dream. What dreams may come? Who was that?

> To sleep, perchance to dream,
> [. . .] for in that sleep of death what dreams may come.

See, I haven't forgotten everything. That's the problem hanging out with an English teacher. He gets inside your head. I've been thinking about the people suffering and the dreams we have at the end, and of the pain involved in getting there. I hear this disease is fairly grim at the end. They always take them away out of quarantine when they start heaving. One of the doctors here, who has worked in Iraq, described the lungs at the end as looking like two bombs had gone off on either side of the chest. Our engine room. Our respiratory system. We give it so little thought from one moment to the next. We have so many words for the heart; heart attack, broken heart, heartache. But very little for the lungs. We don't speak of a lung attack or lung death. Maybe it's because there's two of them. Partners in crime. The lack of a single lungular identity might do it. The lungs working overtime as partners. Breathy lovers swelling and falling. A double-cylinder engine, a twin valve. Silently propelling us with barely a shudder. They're at the root of everything, drawing into the lifeblood the earth's firmament. Our true connection with our environment. Our landbridge. All my environmental activism and I'd forgotten about the lungs. Transmuting the daily bread of air into ever-living breath. Our final connection with our firmament. An elixir right inside our chest. That glorious heaving I used to get running in the open air by the pier. Alchemy working within at every breath. And then this universal pain at losing the breath. The breath that marks our coming and our going. From the primal scream to the rattle in the throat, our life is bookended by its movement. Carry on the wind my words to quicken a new breath. Prayers and thoughts across the miles to all you caught up in this collective gasp for air. Ventilate us all, O gods, for as long as we have lungs to breathe. Let our words caress this breath, this divine intoxicant, this most elemental of connections with our planet. Now, at last, I felt I had a new cause to fight for, a new direction, when I called my district council focus group together again.

John

Lines come back to me when I lie here, waiting for the glimmer of morning. I never know if I have them right. No way to check. No need to know. The way I remember them has its own meaning for me.

> I dream of a Ledaean body, bent
> Above a sinking fire

These lines bring Phoebe back. Oh Phoebe. What was it we shared? Was it a universal need speaking through us? The contrast with what we have now in our isolation is stark. And Sue! Can you ever forgive me? Can you ever take me back? Sometimes I think I catch Phoebe's shadow from our quarantine cell in the lengthening shadows cast on the plasterboard in this old house. They become a companion in my isolation. I try not to let my parents' neighbours know I have returned. There will be recriminations. They will call the Gardaí. Have me quarantined again. Isn't my self-quarantine enough? All I did to travel here and now I can't go out. Gardaí have been given special powers to stop anyone on the streets. They check ID and I don't even have the new ID card.

The familiar places look strange in their emptiness. The Glen Park was always a special place for me. Where I went to jog in the early morning. A true Cork park. The lake waters slowly being reclaimed by sludge and reeds. The mud paths around the lake with barely a hint of gravel. The unkempt borders and ditches. The ruins of the old ascendancy house left overgrown. The half-kilometre, disabled entrance zig-zagging all the way down to the lake, its dark green metal balustrades riven with weeds and grass. The wooden notice boards and wooden benches blackened at the edges by the fires that groups of gatting teenagers light up to keep them entertained as they joyride around the park. One day I found a burnt-out car rammed into the new automatic metal gates of the County Council building in the park grounds.

Now I go there before sun up to jog in the darkness. Coots and mallards scuttle out of the undergrowth off the mud paths as I pass. Sometimes I jump in fright mid-stride and I ask myself if I am more spooked by the stray coots running or by the prospect of not knowing what lies ahead. I have never felt so unmoored. My job is on hold, my marriage is on hold, my health is on hold. My parents ask me why I have returned. Our most basic connections are out of grasp and because they are, we question what they mean to us. Our freedoms are diminished. We can't be seen out. We can't assemble or meet friends. All interaction is virtual and with that all our interaction is under surveillance. A surveillance-state couldn't have dreamed up a better scenario. All small business will fold. All artists will be forced to beg. Universities will close and merge. Students will ask themselves why they are paying 10K, 20K, 60K for what can be done online. And if it's just as good online, why don't we all attend Harvard or Oxford. What's the point of my local college or uni? I get it. I understand how the government and big business will exploit the situation to curb freedoms even when this is all over. Didn't Phoebe give me an earful? It was all she ever spoke about.

But it doesn't hold me. It doesn't keep me awake at night. What keeps me awake at night are the basic human fears and connections that my memory of touch has given me. I fear for my parents' safety for I remember their touch, their embraces. I fear for their safety because I recall the touch of my own wife and boy. I am fearful for their safety. I have provided for them, but I want to be there to protect them. I recall the days at home in Sai Kung with Sue and Sam. Me working at my desk and Sam's cries and constant moans of need from the playpen, moans giving way to desperate guttural chokes. Me, my back to him, writing, letting it continue. Mama, Mama, mhwaah, mhwaaah. Then a cough. Crying. Take me out of here. Take me out of this playpen, this prison. The rattle strung up on the barriers of the pen only clatters like chains against the bars. The long screeches from the throat and the moans for release. And me, at the table a few feet away, writing. Trying to blot out the cries, when all the time I didn't get it. I didn't get how I was the same. The child is the father of the man. These scribbles were my cry. My appeal to the gods of time. My elders. My cry to release us all. Open the gates and the borders, the houses and the pens. I needed to take him up and listen to him. Wasn't it what I had denied myself? Locked up in my own story because I was told it was the way to be. Locking out the cries that I could ease. I could open everything, everything in me to him, right now, inches away, but still I resist. I jerked back to reality and the memory was gone but not the feeling of loss.

Sometimes too I am kept awake by the memory of her touch. It is more real than all I have returned to here and only found absent, unreachable, or empty. We gave ourselves to each other and now separated, perhaps forever, I feel like I never had a more physical experience. The stark contrast with what I have now makes it only stronger.

Phoebe

There is social unrest in Italy and is it any surprise? A man was filmed shouting at police over the bank's opening hours. The bank had closed before he could cash his mother's pension. It was all they had to rely on. He screamed that they had no food or money. Another video posted online had a young Italian father and his son eating a slice of bread. 'It is all we have. I have had enough. A revolution is coming.' They say the videos are being shared by anarchist groups but they're only three weeks into lockdown. When people have no food, they will do all they can for their families. The UK government medic today called for measures to remain in place for six months. I understand the medical plan. I've read all the reports about flattening the curve, herd immunity, and preparing for the peak. But people will not survive. The gig economy made us all live from week to week. We might be able to deal with two weeks, but six months is another story. There will be desperation. Resources will dry up. It is unthinkable what might be coming. We are so slow to adapt to new realities. We are so afraid to imagine life without any social support. Why are people still paying for food? Only to keep supply chains going. But if raiding, stealing and hoarding continue, there will be no supply chain. It will only accelerate. There will be pitched battles. Loss of life. People will scavenge. And once broken, how will supply chains ever get back up and running?

John and I talked about how we felt so much of who we know ourselves to be comes to us unconsciously from every interaction. From every smile and every harsh word. We are forever shaping and reshaping ourselves according to how we experience ourselves through others. Now, with most interactions gone or dramatically altered, what kind of answers were we were coming up with when we asked ourselves the old questions, 'Why am I here?' 'What is my purpose?' Even in the last century after the World Wars, people could come together. There was a new sense of community. Today, everything happens from a distance and with stealth, even when an enemy power invades or an unjust legal system sentences us. Today, we find ourselves capable for the first time of sentencing ourselves. But John talked too much. I knew we needed action. There was still so much to fight for. He looks back at what the books say, but I look forward for the people who voted for me.

They keep blaming us for letting our guard down. I saw something Kwok-ying posted online. He thinks the second wave is down to us letting our guard down. He says we were too quick to let life back in, too quick to let life show itself again. So, the government cut back further. There was no going out. No groups of more than four. No alcohol sales. No restaurants. And yet the numbers rise. What more can they take from us? Is there to be no leaving your bed? No internet use as servers cannot be maintained and they may overheat? In the end, what is the value of the life that is being saved? In the end, what has the virus not taken from us already? A story today tells of the finance official of Germany's wealthiest state killing himself because he was 'deeply worried' about the economic impact of the pandemic. What did he know? How bad was it? He basically ran the coffers of Frankfurt and the headquarters of Germany's two biggest banks, Deutsche Bank and Commerzbank. His body was found dead near a railway track on Saturday. He leaves behind a wife and two children. The most powerful financial official in Europe's strongest economy kills himself because of being 'too worried'. It is no simple recession. What was he thinking on that last walk to the station? Surely, he must have seen buffers, government bail outs, international debt schemes that would have saved countries and people like after the

Great Recession? In Hong Kong the surplus is being drained. It was all Hong Kongers could ever point to in keeping some notion of separation between them and China alive. Hong Kong has a huge surplus, they would say. China wants our surplus. Soon there would be no surplus, only surplus dead.

I walk in the old concrete compound beyond the tower blocks back now in the Fotan quarantine. I had just been found to have low-grade infection again. Another two weeks, minimum. Messages from friends are drying up. I think back to the night we had on Lamma. I think back to the intensity. Despite all the activism and all the ambition, it has become a fulcrum point from which to view my life. I have no personal surge of infection. I can only wait. They say quarantine is now the safest place to be. Both of us then in quarantine, across the miles.

John

W e won't be the first or the last to be here. I've got the memory of other lines coming, other times. I was always fishing for quotes before a class and some of them stuck. The way prisoners suffered. We have their words. I think of both the fictional and the real prisoners. Wilde, Meursault, Mandela. The way they turned it round. The way they transformed it into a beacon for others. How does Wilde put it?

> I have got to make everything that has happened to me good for me. The plank bed, the loathsome food, the hard ropes shredded into oakum till one's finger-tips grow dull with pain.

I had to return. And now I would return again to Hong Kong. Here, I was a refugee between islands of love. An old song called 'The Old House' that my father sang comes back to me.

> Lonely I wander through streets of my childhood . . .

I hear it now as a song about the expat's return to a people who have long gone. Like Oisín returning to his homeland from Tír na nÓg, discovering they have all gone. Like the speaker of the old song 'Spancil Hill' returning to find the 'old ones are all dead and gone, the young are turning grey.' It was everywhere. Ghosts and isolated returnees were everywhere in the songs. Perhaps that's all I was. No more than a ghost. Wasn't it what they called me in Hong Kong? A *gweilo*, a ghost-man. Haunting a people from which I am now twice removed. The expat returns to be invisible. Out of sight, out of mind to the power of two. But they could never have imagined a return like this. Return in real time, in the present, to a family you can't touch. To parents you can only view from a distance. They would have called it black magic. The curse of the banshee.

Who am I fooling with my talk of sacrifice and transformation? The only sacrifice is happening every day at the frontlines. In A and E and ER wards all across the world. What am I doing here? Each morning, I call them and I hear the same sorrow on the phone. I bring groceries to the door only to discover neighbours have brought them already. They have nowhere to put all the food. Their medicines are delivered by the Gardaí every month.

I walk the park one last time. I was deciding to get a flight back. Risk it all again. Would they let me back in at immigration? End my days between borders in the great Transfer Desk in the Sky. If I make it through, it's quarantine again. Only this time they won't put me in Lamma. I won't be seeing Phoebe. I know she's safe. She'll be there to the end of days and beyond. Waiting until the world spins us the right way up. They'll lock me away in one of the new island quarantines. Out where the lepers used to stay. Where they built the old Catholic church. In between Golf Island and the Floating Cemetery, out beyond Yau Tong. But there's no sacrifice in what I do. I've been too obsessed with self-sacrifice to understand it. I've never really felt the need of others deeply enough to be able to do it. I ask myself where the seed was planted. How the sacrificial became mock-heroic. Why I was visited by these scenes of myself being recognized as the last tragic victim of a struggle I had tried with all my might to confront. Sometimes, walking down a street, I'll tear up at the prospect of how others will look on in awe when I am hit by seemingly flattening tragedy. It's an obsession, an unhealthy one. Now, I'm being found out. Now, I'm discovering my perspective was all wrong. Was it the movies

I used to watch with my mother where heroes and heroines sit alone waiting for their sacrifice to be discovered, where they fight together against impossible odds? Yul Bryner in *The Magnificent Seven*, Deborah Kerr waiting on Cary Grant in *An Affair to Remember*, Mr Rochester waiting on Jane Eyre, and then Father Damien in Molokai waiting to be taken away by leprosy. My mother and I had watched the movie of Father Damien together in the old house. The haunting images of disease never left me. I visited his crypt in Saint Anthony's Chapel in Leuven a few years ago when I was there for a conference. There was a big workshop on the Famine. I had sat through it all in frustration wondering how they could still go on about the Famine. It was another time, another place. We don't need reminding of it I said. I argued that Ireland needs to move on from death and disease, to give up this philosophy of loss. I even claimed that language itself in Ireland was understood in terms of loss. All because of the Famine. The panellists and the audience looked on unmoved. They didn't seem to get behind me. I sat back and listened to the next panel from the back of the room. One of the speakers seemed a little flippant when he was talking about how the Famine and all that death and disease should be remembered. My back was up. I felt annoyed, piqued even. Was I changing my tune so soon? I was amazed at how fickle I was. Now, all I wanted to do, was to leap to the defence of those who had been going on about the importance of Famine commemoration. But I had to come at it from a different angle so I wouldn't appear to be contradicting myself. I raised my hand for one last comment.

- 'Do you think it's time for us to start thinking about putting on a version of Famine: The Musical?'

A few might have smirked. Some might even have rolled their eyes. I couldn't wait any longer for the coffee-break, so I left the classroom and took a walk outside. At the end of the road I saw a small church. It ended up being the chapel where Father Damien was buried. Death and disease were following me around Leuven. Now, today, as I wait here in quarantine in Cork, I hear Belgium has one of the highest death rates in the world for the virus. But these are only tables, and no one believes them. I remember that walk to Father Damien's chapel. I went down to the crypt. The blown up black and white photo of Damien with his face clearly riddled with leprosy always turned my stomach. But I still got more of an emotional hit from how I imagined myself to be a kindred spirit, one who could also play his major role in life as a victim of flattening tragedy. Only now do I see how off my emotional compass was. Helping others required skills I did not possess in such abundance. Instead of sensationalizing charity and care, I needed to act. I needed to forget about my obsession with playing the victim and to get out there, to help the real victims. I was feeling as if the return had not been useless. At least I was feeling a change in how I thought. The hard part now was to follow through. The burning need, the sense of urgency to perform the simple acts that would help the lives I could, rushed through me as if a valve had been opened. I would return to Sue and my sick boy.

John and Sue

I rose one morning in the dark and decided to see some of my old haunts one last time. I knew now I was leaving Ireland. I had tried to help. There was one family here I would always struggle to touch and live with for any great length of time and another across the miles with which I had the chance to rediscover touch. The two could never come together. Not now with all the sickness about, with the restrictions on travel, and with the recriminations rising towards people of Chinese ethnicity. I had made a decision because I had to. Thinking about it tears me apart, but staying in this half-way house, slinking around in the dark like a fugitive, was helping no one.

I walked down Summer Hill past the old toll house at St Luke's. I remembered the long nights of heartache on the payphones down near the corner shop now long gone. I passed the off-licence and then St Patrick's Church with the steps down to Lower Glanmire Road. I had my own first confession story from the church, the same church Frank O'Connor made famous. I continued down past the old Coliseum and over Brian Boru Bridge. I recalled the nights of despair walking half-drunk over this bridge, feeling that the dark Lee waters would never let me go. Their green, suppurating waters, still stinking after the big drainage works, always seemed to be washing me in again on their easy, rolling tides. Then on down to the South Mall, the street of auctioneers and bankers, where I'd go as a teenager with a hand-written note on Basildon Bond paper from my father to ask the bank manager for money for the week ahead only to be turned

away to another few days without food. Then out on to the Grand
Parade, Cork's promenade near the river, the big sycamores lining
the wide junction. Once I used to live in the top floor of the tallest
building on this street with my French girlfriend and her Malaysian
flatmate. We had a view right down the Western Road to the gates
of the college. The college looked to me like a protected fortress
when I used to pass its tall railings as a child on the number eight
bus. I crossed over to Liberty Street and cut through Cornmarket
Street for the millennium footbridge. The gulls were gathered
around the old sewage pipe that led into the river. I'm no better
than them, I thought. A scavenger for attention.

I needed to remember these streets. I needed to get my mind
off this virus. I took a left on Pope's Quay and came to the Lee Taxi
shelter. I passed through the shortcut behind the Off-Licence and
started climbing Shandon Street. There were shops here that were
over a hundred years old. Handed down from father to son and
from father to daughter. They sold everything from boiled sweets
to tripe. The butchers up here still sold rabbit and eel. There were
shoe shops that had groceries in the back and electrical shops that
doubled-up as taxi ranks. The boundaries blurred on Shandon
Street. It was old Cork. It was not what you sold or what you
knew about it but how you sold it and who you knew. The African
and Polish shops fitted right in with their cheap interior decor and
family approach. Everyone helped each other out and any service
could be found if you knew who to ask. Sue liked this part of the
city. She told me stories about growing up in Hong Kong and how
bits of Shandon reminded her of some of it. Of her grandfather's
old printing shop in the side streets of Hong Kong island and
of her father's locksmith shop in Mongkok. She remembered as
a child climbing the steep streets to her grandfather's shop. The
street was so steep and the buildings so narrow they had to run
the shop across two adjoining buildings. Some of the old printing
machines were so big that, when they knocked through the walls
between the buildings, the printing machine's left side ended up

being on a different level to its right side. Her grandfather called it
the little lady. In summer, they'd leave the doors open to the street.
She remembered the smell of the black ink like tar and the rubber
rollers racing in the heat. Sometimes, when the machines were
shut off and when her grandfather wasn't looking, she liked to
rest the side of her face against the warm rubber of the rollers. She
felt a warmth run through her that was comforting and exciting.
At lunch time, she'd run to the stall selling dim sum and bring
her grandfather back his *chau siu bau* wrapped in old newspaper.
When her father peeled off the newspaper, she could see some of
the old newsprint had been transferred to the soft white bread of
the dumpling. Words being eaten with the meat. Grandad sucked
on the straw of his *dung lai cha* and all the time I was wondering
where all this paper went. Who could read so many characters?
Shandon Street reminded her of her old Hong Kong. There
were no airs and graces. People simply did business. Business was
the life blood, and it didn't matter how you did it so long as you
respected business itself.

We could've done so much here. Who knows? Had a family,
started a business. Wasn't Sue as innovative as they come? Didn't
she make a small business out of a few bags of feathers and a
selection of old fabric? Why didn't I ever see the reality until it
was too late? It took this sickness to remind me what was within
my grasp all along. It took that night with Phoebe. The power
of touch and how we were afraid of it. Afraid of it until we knew
it was endangered. We're only given so many chances, so many
characters to get it right.

John

As I'm boarding the plane in Dublin, I recall some memories with my father from the previous summer, from the days before the virus. I turn back and breathe in the air before I ascend the stairs into the plane. The queue ahead of me is moving slowly. I still have time. I'm back in a moment from only last summer when my father and I had painted the wall outside the house together.

My father was born in Beara under Hungry Hill. He used to tell us stories of riding on his mother's bike to Allihies in the '30s and '40s to see her mother's sister, Kathleen, before she met Jack and sailed for Walthamstow. They used to climb the base of Hungry Hill together to see her father up beyond Páirc Mhór and Páirc Bheag and Páirc Theas and Laighnea. Each field had a name since the Famine. The hill itself was a reminder of the Great Hunger. Would there be Covid hospitals and Covid burial grounds after this virus has passed? Or Covid Mountain? Back in my father's day, places and fields had personalities. Maybe it was something we needed to bring back. The people knew what could happen if the fields were slighted. They called the land the hungry grass. To remember all the death and disease. My father told me his grandfather threw old dogs into the sea off Rosmacowen pier, down where the waters rode to Beare Island. Tied rocks to them and threw them in the Atlantic. My brothers and I used to hunt under rocks on Pairc Mhor for the biggest insects we could find on summer holidays down to West Cork. Cruel times my father told us. He'd still wince in the Mayfield sitting room, remembering his grandfather beating a badger to death with the face of a shovel.

My father said the old cottage called Bank first had only sackcloths for walls—the cottage where my father was born ten years after independence. His father, Michael, would be out all weather with the sandboat. No running water in the house. Grass and dock leaves in the fields aplenty. Michael and his cousins would be dredging the bottom of the sea for good sand for the fields. The fertilizer and sea weed left on shore and dragged up the coast road past the fuchsia and nettle. All under the watchful eye of Hungry Hill. My father was telling me how his own grandfather, Michael's father, Mortimer—Murt they called him—had gout. He had a bad leg. A small stocky man with a bad leg and an untidy beard. Like it was covering something. A scar. A childhood illness. A harelip. He had a phrase he always used, 'My pocket thinks my hand is mad.' He said it every time my father went looking for coins from him and my father repeated it to us. Murt's father, Tim, lived through the Famine and so he had my great-grandfather late. It affected him growing up they said. The stories shared round the firesides at night. He could be excused for the gout. Hadn't he made it through *and* stayed put? We had one photo of Murt out in the trees behind the house sitting on a small stool. His eyes going at the camera like it were some wild animal. Why the photo out there? In the middle of the forest? They got him all dressed up in his Sunday suit and made him limp out. Sat him on the old stool. The suit exploding on him. Was it a special spot for him? Had something happened there? In those woods? I could never have imagined there was any connection between old man Murt and this place out here, between Murt and Hong Kong. It was the last thing I could ever have imagined. It was only when I did some research that I could piece it all together. It helped me see my journey to Hong Kong as in some way written in the stars.

I discovered that in the county elections the year Murt's father, Tim, got the old cottage that the local politicians had promised Tim money for trees around his house in their eleven acres. They were still shipping lumber off to the UK. In the

UK parliament elections, his family had supported a man called Hennessy. Hennessy was the right man for Ireland. John Pope Hennessy. The name had godliness riven through it. Stand up for Cork to those bastards in London town. Hennessy'd get the job done. Hennessy'd help get them independence. Wasn't he Cork-born and raised? Studied in the college too. Medicine they said. He'd even come down to Beara in a trap one summer to meet the people. Murt stood beside his father, Tim, in Castletownbere Mart one Wednesday morning when Hennessy came down as a Conservative member of the UK parliament. Hennessy came up to Tim and Murt looked on at his father's side. Murt said he remembered him as a small, wiry man. With a hooked nose. Kept his chin up high. A lot of airs and graces. Wasn't he only John Pope Hennessy, the future governor of Hong Kong? I never stopped telling Sue about it. It knocked me for six when I made the connection. There they were discussing calves and trees in West Cork in the 1860s. Murt's father, Tim, was trying to get him to promise to do something about the trees:

-   'Sure, you'll remember us down here. Ryans of Beara. Leaders of the British East India Company. I'm telling ye,' said Murt's father.
-   'Getaway out o' that now. Don't be coddin' me!' Hennessy had fired back.
-   'I'm telling ye. The whole truth. My own cousin Laurence, son of Philip the blacksmith, sure wasn't he the Guardian of the British East India Company? Got the whole thing going out foreign.' Murt's father couldn't stop smirking, scratching his dirty beard, thinking back on it. 'The Guardian of the British East India Company I'm telling ye and he came from these fields.'

Hennessy smiled and backed away. Maybe a thought crossed his mind. What was there out there? Beyond Castletownbere and

the Rosmacowen pier. Out beyond the Atlantic. Out there in the
East? He came to and smiled back at Murt's father.

-   'Well we'll make sure there's no British West Cork Company,
    won't we now?'

Yes, Hennessy was the right man for Ireland. In the end, he lost out
the second time round by seven votes. He spent a year appealing it.
Even his friends Disraeli, Napoleon III, and the Emperor Francis
Joseph couldn't change the result. He went into hiding of a kind
with his debt and fathered two children by a mistress. Next they
heard, he was going away foreign. Off to rule over the Chinese
they said. Another one gone. Murt could never forgive him. He
took it to heart. Couldn't he wait around? Turning his back on his
people. We were good enough for him when he needed our vote.
    It was in the United College Library Archives of *Chungman
Daiho* that I stumbled upon Hennessy's letters about Cork.
Hennessy had sent some of them from Cork shortly after he met
my great-grandfather. Then I read the letters he sent from Hong
Kong in the 1880s about his time in Cork during the Famine.
About those days when him and Murt's father were eating the
hungry grass and seeing their neighbours and families die of
hunger. In another time, but surrounded again by death and
disease. What *had* happened in those forests? Why did Murt need
to have the photo taken there? Hennessy's speech on the Famine
given at Peddars Wharf in Hong Kong on 06 March 1880 was still
given for the Irish Distress Fund. It took them that long to get over
it. That long to change their ways. It was the same week that he
had refused to send a seventeen-year-old, Chinese young-offender
back to another famine in the mainland. As he spoke on the pier,
with the wind ruffling his fair curls, Hennessy remembered those
days in Cork. Long before Murt was put on that stool in that
clearing in the forest behind the old house. Hennessy's words to
the assembled Chinese and European dignitaries about a place

they may never have heard of were all that stood between them
and a good *dim sum*:

-   '. . . perhaps there are few present who actually remember
    the events of the Great Famine of 1846 and 1847. I am
    sorry to say that I am old enough to remember them and,
    though I was only twelve years of age at the time, I have a
    vivid recollection of the fact that I then saw in the streets
    of Cork one morning seven dead bodies lying not far from
    the residence of my father, a sight which has remained ever
    engraved on my memory. They were in two groups: one, a
    group of five people lying dead, and another of two, a woman,
    apparently a young woman, and what appeared to me to be a
    very old but diminutive woman, but on looking closely, I saw
    that it was in reality a dead child; it had died of starvation . . .'

Murt's father would still be there in Bank, waiting, when Hennessy
came back years later to run against Parnell's man in 1890. I can
imagine how he saw the returning Hennessy. *That Hennessy has
some neck. Comes back from feckin' China to run against the last High
King of Ireland. The Saviour of Ireland. Beats Parnell's man by a
single vote. It killed Parnell.* Hennessy ended up destroying Parnell,
Murt used to say. 'My Dead King' Joyce would write about Parnell
a few years later. What goes around comes around. Me boarding
a plane, leaving one disease-stricken version of Ireland, as I recall
a different time when Hennessy left Hong Kong to return to an
Ireland he had always associated with disease. It's a cycle of sorts.
Wheels within wheels. Joyce would have had a field day. What he
would call 'our wholemole millwheeling vicociclometer'.

    But I know I'm getting distracted again. Keep to the job in
hand. Focus on what you can do for Sue and your sick boy. Then,
as the plane takes off and I'm getting emotional about this last
departure from a diseased land, I'm back again in the sunshine of
the previous summer in our Cork driveway.

A memory of my father hits me. I need to remember what
he did for us as I commit to my own role as a father. This time
I'm taking a five-litre tub of white masonry paint out to the old
pebbledash wall a few doors down from Hennessy's old home. It's
early summer from only a few years ago. It's a dividing wall between
us and the neighbours in Dillons Cross. The wall is no bigger than a
child. Waist high on our side, chest high on the neighbours'. Some
cowboy builders sold me the lie that the wall was saturated. Told
me the garden was soaking up water and that the water was running
into the wall's foundations. I never did get the builder's real name.
'Mick' he said to call him. Never a surname. Later on, my friends
said they were the Hanleys, a family well-known for hassling elderly
couples in the area. Others say they were from Ballyvolane. I recall
how they operated. How they got work from me. Mick is standing
at the wall, his face a dirty brown, his belly tight under the faded
navy polo-shirt. His hair a tight, frizzy brown.

- 'Didn't yer neighbour Thomas feckin' put up those concrete
  supports on his side. Too afraid to come near ye so he was.
  Sure didn't he think you were a bit uppity. C'mere to me.
  I don't like to be saying now but sure it's the word around.
  They never feckin' see ye. You're always away foreign. The
  only solution. Lose the garden.'
- 'You're saying I should lose the whole thing?'
- 'The whole feckin' thing. It's feckin' saturated. It's a feckin'
  sponge.'

He walks down to the end of the path and stares down the narrow
hill as if he's waiting for something. He kicks a bit of loose
concrete on the path with his worn work boot, already destroying
our property.

- 'Are ye married out there?'
- 'I am, yes.'

-   'To a foreign girl?'
-   'Yes, a Hong Kong woman.'
-   'Would she come back? Back here?'
-   'Well, we're discussing it. The plan was ye see . . .'
-   'Would ye leave her if she wouldn't?'
-   'Well . . .'

No one has ever asked me that. I try to get back on track.

-   'So it's four for the path, is it?'
-   'Ah, John, John. Don't be coddin' me.'

Before I respond, he moves down along the path, the tongues on his open caterpillar boots flapping. He stops in front of the house. He starts picking a bit of the loose pebbledash off the front wall.

-   'See that? D'ye see that? The rain gets in there now, freezes and pushes out the plaster. All has to be replaced. We could do a job for ye on that. Skim the whole lot. Scaffold up here. Scaffold there. I'm telling ye. Do the path and the front o' the house. You won't know yerself.'
-   'So, ye said it was four for the path.'
-   'John, I'm telling ye, don't be coddin' me now. Are ye feckin' serious? Are ye? Ten for the path and garden. Are ye feckin' serious?'
-   'Ten? You said four yesterday. There's no way I can do that. That's way beyond what ye told me. Look we better stop the whole thing.'

He starts leaning on the plaster of the house. He's looking down at the ground as if he's steadying himself.

-   'Look it. John. John. I'm not coddin' ye. I'm going through a feckin' divorce. The bitch left me. Took a house for a millun.

Brand new house for a millun. Broke me back so it did. Left
me with the six kids.'
-      'I'm sorry. I'm sorry to hear it. It must be a real shock.'

He starts moving off again down the path towards the road.

-      'I'm off, John. Big job down in Ballyvolane. Tomorra!'

With the phone pushed into his big, sweating head he's already
walking backwards down the hill.

-      'Seamus, will ye feckin' tell them I'm coming?'

We haven't agreed anything and there's a lump off my front wall
and my path. Before we could talk again, they had a JCB digger in
the driveway and half the garden dug out.
      Now I'm going out with the tin of paint the first sunny day in
May. Rain clouds start gathering with half the wall still to paint.
Gusts of wind pass along the wall buffeting the dust cloth pinioned
to the driveway with the five spare paving blocks they left behind.
The sun spears the clouds and the new coat of white suddenly
lights up. I'm enjoying the novel sensation of warm Cork sunshine
when my father joins me.

-      'Painting is relaxing. I'm like you, Dad, painting the huge
       gable wall in Mayfield each year.'
I say it again thinking I might have been unclear.
-      'I'm like you, Dad, painting that huge gable wall in Mayfield
       each year.'
-      'What's that? What wall? Sorry. No. Sorry.'
-      'That big wall you used to paint every few years with a five-
       inch brush. You painted it cream.'

He stares down at the base of the wall, trying to recover some
vague memory of what I describe. He looks up again as if to admit

defeat. His eyes weary. It's as if he's been accepting his memory is not what it was for a long time.

- 'I'm sorry. No.'

I try to make as little of it as possible.

- 'Do you want to do a section? Do the top. Mind your clothes. I need to stand up for a second.'

I hand him the brush. I wanted to get Dad thinking about all the painting he'd done all through his life. In the houses in Sidcup, Bray, Glanmire, Mayfield, Montenotte. I give him the brush. He steps forward and takes it up. He's slow to start, but then he's dancing with the brush, drawing it back and forth in wide brushstrokes with great flair and skill. He's like the expert I knew he was, his strokes getting more pronounced. Soon the top of the wall is all finished. I can see the relief on his face. Surely he's reliving the feeling of having painted before. Maybe he even remembered that wall in Mayfield. And then he says something that tells me it's coming back. That gable wall. It was a wall I kept returning to because of Dad's perseverance in a housing estate where we were picked on because we were different. One Halloween we kept all the lights off round the house so the boys of the estate wouldn't think we were inside. So I go back to Dad working the long hours on that wall as a gesture of defiance. Knowing there would be graffiti on it in the morning. Him at the top of the wooden ladder, his back to the whole estate. Silver Heights Avenue falling away behind him to the valley below and the long road down to Tivoli and Silver Springs. He's coming in after a long day of painting with spots of cream all through his auburn hair and across his face and hands, like marks of battle. The hairs of the five-inch brush in his hand are curved like a scimitar from the shape of the wall and the hard yards of pebbledash. Now, as I watch him paint our wall at Dillons Cross, I'm sad for the memory he couldn't recall straight off. Maybe it's a memory only I have now, a memory breaking free from the clutches of collective memory even as I harness it here to the page and run it into the ground until it sticks. What happens when memories that bind us die? Does part of me also die off with a memory no longer shared? Time comes along like the JCB of those cowboy builders. I can see Mick now in the driver's seat. His feral passion driving the jaws of the digger into the rich soil of our garden. Prestige Paving they called themselves. Time comes along like them and piston drives the century-old loamy sods apart, reducing them to mounds of black soil, cracked concrete slab, and weed ready only for compost for another man's garden.

IV

Hong Kong
July–October, 2020

John

It's different here now since quarantine and since I've returned from Ireland. I'm on my own. Sue took Sam and moved back into her mum's place. I don't know how I could have expected her to wait. All through my extended quarantine and then through the time spent in Cork and then another two weeks of quarantine when I came back. But I know it's only temporary. We've been through too much together. It's taken some adapting since Sam came along, but I wouldn't change it for the world.

Sometimes I go back to the benches outside the 24-hour McDonald's. They've taken nearly all the seats away inside for social distancing. Each time I enter, they take my temperature. It ranges from 33.6 to 35.4. I should be in hospital with hypothermia. The woman at the door waves the temperature gun about and sometimes it's aimed at my forehead. Sometimes at my nose or my hair. But there's no getting past it. Once you've stopped and acknowledged her command, once you've given in to the charade, you can enter. These rules don't come from McDonald's or from the government. It's a kind of people power. It's as if they're collectively shouting: 'Look, we're doing it for your own good. For your own safety. Stay healthy! Don't ask questions. Just obey. It's all for your own good. This is not really about your health. Don't you know that? It's a training in compliance. You fool! How could you not know this? You see, soon there won't be any more questions and if you disobey, the gun touching your cool forehead won't be a plastic temperature gun but the cold steel variety.'

Phoebe was definitely having an influence on me! This was the kind of thing she would say. But she'd take it further: "And the confessions, yes, you've noticed them. 'Where have you been?' 'Who have you met?' Soon they will not be scribbled outside a 24-hour McDonald's or an old public housing complex, but in a cold, concrete bunker where you will long for the freedom of the charade, the freedom of the game that was only started to save you from others and from yourself."

"Can't you see this yet? Are you that stupid? It's not to protect you from a virus that we do this. Why would we ever do this when there's no virus in Hong Kong. Well, not one that kills people since no one has died for months. No, it's a training, you fool. A training to teach you how to protect yourself from yourself. All the great campaigns for successful conformism start like this. You should know. You call yourself a teacher, an educator. First, we work on the small things. The coming and the going. The daily confrontation with doors and elevator buttons. First, we sow confusion. Then, pretty soon, you won't be certain how to open a door, commission a lift. You will recall how it all began. A priceless legislative about-turn. In a matter of months, if you think back, we went from a full ban on masks to a state decree that made mask-wearing virtually compulsory. I mean you couldn't have made it up, could you?'

Kwok-ying

The Party announces the opening-up of Wuhan. Carnie is on the case. Wuhan will open. Trains took millions out of Wuhan as soon as they could leave. No one tracked and traced the exodus. Hong Kong awaits. It's a few hours on the speed train from Wuhan. Carnie is on the case. Hong Kong welcomes with open arms her stranded brothers and sisters. Only yesterday Lim announced limited opening of bars and pubs in Hong Kong. At the press conference she deliberated: 'Yes, you can have a drink in a pub. By all means. But no live music and NO dancing.' Not even to 'do the Hazmat'? It seems not. The top student of a Catholic girls' school has spoken. Wuhan now is fifteen days without a local infection. We are bombarding all channels with the news. Tourism into Wuhan will never recover. Mao's Lakeside Retreat will remain a Retreat. No one swims in his lake. The mummified concubines of Marquis Yee of Zheng in the Wuhan Museum have no viewers. We await Carnie's word as all Hong Kongers await her gift of 10,000 HKD. On that day, there will be no virus but there will also be no dancing.

An Instagram post emerged of Carnie at her desk. It was put beside photos of the Queen and Shi at their desks. Family photos were carefully arranged beside and behind the Queen and Shi. One could clearly see the Queen's grandchildren and great-grandchildren. Even one or two of her own children. Shi proudly shows off photos of his family, of himself with his wife and daughter. Carnie, too, has her photos. Arranged carefully on her desk are three photos of Carnie. Carnie as secretary, Carnie as secretary and Carnie as secretary. Carnie is on the case.

Phoebe

My infection has eased. The temperature has dropped. They know how to use their temperature guns here. I've finally got back to my small flat above the district councillor's office on Fuk Man Street. I have so much to organize. The Occupy leader is released Saturday. 300 days in prison in a city under lockdown. Will he notice any difference when he gets out? We have a banner ready. In the end, we had to stick with what was tried and trusted. Six Demands, Not One Less. Free HK. We will stand outside the gates of Pik Uk Prison—where they once made you lick urine off urinals as a rite of passage—and unfurl our banner. It's an important release for the movement. I remember videos of Mandela's raised fist in his walk to freedom in 1990. The drawn, haggard faces of the Birmingham 6. Will we ever have our day in the sun? The government has increased public gatherings to eight. Any more than that and we'll be arrested outside Pik Uk Prison. 'Sustainable protesting' we can call it. 'It's okay. We can walk to our holding cells from here. No need for the paddy wagon.'

It's the online trolling and harassment that gets to you sometimes. You accept a friend request from a local citizen and next minute they're throwing all kinds of abuse at you. Western sausage-eater. Inventing affairs you and your partner had with those in the movement. I've slept with everyone in the pro-democracy camp bar Claudia. But throw enough shit and some of it will stick. The harassment is everywhere. They target academics, politicians, even western shops. Disenfranchised, HK-educated mainland graduates trolling for their country. Okay, I know our side has gone overboard too but what can we do when no one listens. The online cheers when a police officer was infected. The restaurants serving new dishes to celebrate the news. *Saam man yun dan fan*, which translates as both 'barbecued egg and eel on rice' and 'the end for all 30,000 police officers'.

No one knows what to believe. The end of history, they told us, was over thirty years ago. The end of history as bloodshed and irrational power games. We were all supposed to have banished history. We had reached a steady state of reason and had dispensed with history on the way. Didn't we have communicative reason and liberal democracies? What need did we have of history? But history, like art, waits for no one. With so much uncertainty, I'm beginning to doubt my own past. The reminders I get from Facebook and Instagram have been compromised and with them my memories. No sooner do I remember a tender moment, dim sum with my mother, hotpot with my family, the buns my sister bought me on the way to school on Hennessy Road, and I'm thinking of my mother's last words to me about a text she received from a cousin or aunt about the latest harassment. I have taken myself off social media. I'm a politician who can't be political. Both virtual and face-to-face meetings are denied me.

John

There's no way I can see her now. I'm stepping on thin ice. Our quarantine was our time out of time. I sometimes wonder if it ever really happened. The old, unfinished housing complex with the tiles still missing from the concrete floors. And no surveillance. It was a quarantine from the surveillance and self-checking of everyday life. The Social Credit System is working here already. Why did we think good deeds done for the Party in Hong Kong could not be reported in the party log books back across the border? For the thousands commuting every day? Good deeds know no borders. Social cohesion knows no borders.

Yesterday, I had to go into hospital. Sam hit me full in the eye with his hammer when I called over to see him and Sue at her mother's place. I leaned down, while carrying him, to pick up a nappy from the lower shelf of the changing table. Couldn't see my pupil for the blood in my eye. I had to queue outside on the street for the temperature checks to get into the hospital. Then the gun to the forehead. The staring, accusatory eyes of the nurse. A *gweilo*. A likely threat. Put that gun against his forehead a second time.

After the second temperature station, I awaited my turn. I finally got to the check-in counter. Then the next temperature check and blood pressure check. The nurse penetrated me six times, pushing the plastic proboscis hard into my ear cavity, searching for a reading. No one had ever entered me there with such violence. The violations of lockdown? Each time she withdrew the plastic tip, I recoiled, ready to brace for the next penetration. Each time

172

she disposed of the plastic heads in a medical waste bin, she looked scornfully at the reading on her gun. Still no reading. She expected nothing less. She spoke English with the slightly harsh tones that told me she was from the mainland. *Gweilo*s were simply hardwired to upset the system. Wasn't this proof? My thoughts were running like this as she reloaded. This was what I had become. Some kind of paranoid android. Sitting here taking the abuse, bracing myself for it, yet knowing there was something wrong in this constant violation of my person. I even apologized. Can you believe it? I apologized to her for the lack of a reading as she entered me for a sixth time. I had internalized some kind of *gweilo* stereotype in my head and every time I failed to fit in or move through the system without a hitch, I recalled this little *gweilo* man inside, this stubborn monolingual drama queen, and tried to remind myself not to be like him. The more I tried to adapt to fit in, joining dinner parties with my Hong Kong wife and child, taking Cantonese classes, looking out for my local students, the more I became conscious of the gulf that separated us. Try as hard as I might, I could not change their unwillingness to accept me as anything like a local. Each time, I added more detail to the *gweilo* stereotype inside, until it looked more and more like me. In the end, I took some kind of masochistic pleasure in counting the ways I matched the stereotype and grew less eager to discredit it.

The nurse came again. This time I tried humour.

- 'I'm beyond temperature checks.'

I even said it with a smile beneath my mask. But the look she gave me only made the sweating, ruddy, thick-set *gweilo* inside howl all the harder.

Phoebe

It all started because of the boredom of quarantine. The days of isolation. No physical person to talk to. We had spoken once before on election day. I never remembered it, but he remembered coming up to me outside the secondary school where he voted. I was handing out flyers. And then there were the times he saw me getting a coffee in McDonald's. This new Coffee Dock in quarantine was our lifeline. We recognized each other. After eye conversations over a couple of weeks, we spoke, and he said something once as he passed by that really struck a chord:

- 'I see you come here often'
- 'Not much choice'
- 'There's a nice Italian place down the road. It has great views of the ocean. If you go there at sundown you can catch the rays dancing off lovers locked in each other's arms.'

I knew he'd been thinking about it for days. It wasn't even that funny. But the image hit me in the gut. Without a warning, I had this physical yearning. For something that was so normal. And yet I'd almost responded to him with a look of shock and disapproval. All I could do was smile behind my mask. He passed by again a few days later, and we spoke again from the required two metres apart, fully face-masked, and only when the security guards had their backs to us. Something about speaking from two metres away made everything into a performance. At the very least your voice had to carry. And then how did you say something from such a distance and not let the guards hear you? It was impossible. What you said had to be short and yet it had to leave the listener with the feeling she had been in a much longer conversation. So, he worked on his lines just as he had worked on those lines he told me he once put in his journals in the 24-hour McDonald's in Sai Kung. Then, one day, I drop my number on a piece of paper beside his table as I was leaving. The texts were a way of getting through the quarantine:

NICE TO SEE YOU TODAY

U2

JUST HAD TO TALK TO A BODY I CAN SEE

YES, BODIES ARE SCARCE THESE DAYS.

LIVING ONES. WITHIN REACH

GOOD BODIES?

ANYBODY!

VILE BODIES

FAT BODIES

FULL BODIES

WARM BODIES

WE SOUND LIKE ZOMBIES!

BUT THAT'S HOW I FEEL!

A ZOMBIE?

I CRAVE WARM FLESH

;) DID YOU SEE ZOMBIE GOT TO 1 BILLION PLAYS? ONLY THE 6TH SONG EVER

EVERYONE'S FEELING IT!

ALL THOSE PRE-COVID ZOMBIE FLICKS

THEY KNEW IT WAS COMING

SO WHAT KIND R U?

OF ZOMBIE?

YEAH

HAZMAT ZOMBIE OBVIOUSLY. U?

CORPSE ZOMBIE—YUNNO FROM WARM BODIES—STILL SOME MENTAL CAPACITIES LEFT FOR TEXTING ;)

WE SHOULD BREAK THE ZOMBIE RULES
How so? buy 2 McDonald's 24x7 coffees?
Very good but we should
Be 2 zombies 2 each other?

No, warm bodies
OK, I got a plan

For what? To break the rules?
Yeah

2 FINGERS TO THE ZOMBIE RULES
OH YEAH
MEET IN ONE OF OUR ROOMS

they'd spot us
maybe, maybe not. it's only more isolation
I've been infected so long and you too yeah?
Yeah we're the long tails—slow burning
We've zombified covid ;)

ok, but one condition
what?

My room
No prob. mine is a little dull

Phoebe

Hong Kong life was always a kind of lockdown when you come to think about it. The densely packed towers of close-knit public housing. The five of us in 300 square feet. My bed beside the cooker. Doing my homework through all those years on the kitchen table. The lack of space meant there were rules about how to learn to confine yourself. Swinging a cat, if you were allowed one, would have been a kind of fantasy.

Then the school, like a penitentiary, at the end of the block. The floors of identical corridors and classrooms rising around a central concrete courtyard where we all took our breaks in uniform under the surveillance of the teachers. In the second school that I went to, there was no room for a playground, so they put it on the roof. It had a huge metal railing all around it. I was too scared to go anywhere near that railing until I was in grade three so I stayed in the locked classroom for every break.

I guess we were more prepared than most. But we made it our world and we were none the worse for it. Children imagine dreams into the smallest spaces. The space of the cot becomes a world for dolls and trolls. They fight it out on the narrow strip of blanket. Good fighting bad. It was always what I played at. The long walks along the streets of North Point in the humid days of summer. The smells of the *gai see* and the pork butchers with the red lanterns hanging low over the cuts of pork. Dead meat. It was always something I associated with the red lights I found down by Temple Street or near Yau Ma Tei. I could never get it out of my mind.

Come to think of it, the main difference between Hong Kong and many other big cities is that the streets and the parks are all your world most of the time. I have no memory there of long train journeys across days with the countryside changing outside your window as fields and villages speed by. Or of day-long car journeys that make you forget where you started. Like the trips I took on the bus with Bill in Ireland going from Cork to Westport and from Cork to Sligo. But that was another life. We did have our ferry trips to Macau and our glorious day-long hikes in the country parks. The world beyond Hong Kong was our world too. We didn't see geographical limitations like most other people. Without a solid home of our own, everywhere and elsewhere became places we could lay claim to, if only in our imaginations.

Kwok-ying

Gold is the only option. Even the daily report on the real-time value of my new Tai Po apartment has stagnated. I was up about 0.5 million only a few weeks ago. Now, it's been hovering, and it even slid back a few days in a row last week. Gold was down to 12,000 HKD for a small bar last week. Slim pickings for all the cash I gave them. One guy came away with a rucksack full of the stuff. He won't be hiking anywhere with that. Got my safe installed. Put it beside my bed. With GDP down 8.9 per cent, they've nearly bled us dry. Friends are moving pension stocks from HK options to US options. I don't know. I can't go anywhere else. If the economy tanks, I have my gold. A mini bar every pay check. Now, that's something to live for. By the end of the year I can fill a cigarette pack. My gold fingers. They'd never expect them to be there. Leave the pack lying around the apartment. They can ransack the safe then for all I care. Even my mother is worried. Every time I call her, all she says is, 'Don't buy, Don't buy, Don't buy.' Each month, on pay day, I join the queue at the Lee Cheong Gold Dealers Ltd. in Sheung Wan. I might even splash out on one of those gold pigs with all the teats for weddings that they have in the windows of Luk Fuk Jewellery. Marriage gifts I know, but I might never get married if this keeps up.

Phoebe

John had this theory about us all. He said he'd been researching
it for years. 'Cloneliness' he called it. Something about how we
were all being reproduced as online lonely clones by big business.
I thought it was batty. He had been reading up on it (the things
those academics waste their time on). Good job no one can get
into the universities now. Last time I visited, there was barbed
wire all around the outer walls of the university and security
guards on every corner and entrance. It was harder to get into than
Pik Uk Prison. So maybe he had a point in one sense. Anyone
working in there must be feeling pretty lonely these days. And
those offices must make them feel a bit like clones. Teaching on
record to voiceless, faceless blanks at the same time each week.
But John was stubborn. He persevered. Said he found evidence for
it all in art from all over. Good luck to him. He said the Japanese
were particularly good at nurturing it. *Hikikomori* he called it. An
extreme form of withdrawal. I'd heard about some of them here.
Those computer kids who can't even take a toilet break after days
online and end up doing themselves all kinds of damage. He was
convinced he was on to something. Then the virus hit, and everyone
was stuck at home, self-isolating. The laptop was our only point
of contact. Our last point of connection with everyone. Locked in,
we needed the laptop to breathe. Locked in, we would surely have
lost so many more without the virtual connection. And he said
he'd never seen it coming. Those years spent researching how the
virtual world makes us all lonely clones and never a thought for
how a pandemic might change things. Bingo. Talk about sticking

your head in the sand. I'm not saying we're not all messed up by the hours online, but what else do we have now? And who knows how long we might need it?

When he touched me, I could feel that loneliness. Like he wasn't able to jump from the virtual to real flesh and blood. He was like a baby put in a bath of water for the first time. A toddler that stands there with the bubbles bobbing at his thighs not knowing what to feel or do. It's like the water's not there. Only the appearance of something new about the legs. A new feeling. In a few minutes, he'll reach out, touch it, and start to move the water about with his hand. Then you see the slow dawning of realization. This is a new element, a new part of my environment.

It was the same with John. When he held my shoulders and pulled me close it was as if he had to remind himself to focus on the sensation. The way his face checked itself and the body paused and then the unsteady motion rising to an almost painfully repetitive grasping. I had to tell him to ease off. He was either not there through shock or through the impassioned intent to make himself feel.

And it wasn't the first time. I've forgotten how many men and women give off that same uncertainty when bodies come in contact or become a zone of possibility in our encounters. Bill was older and he hadn't grown up looking at screens. He was the only one I ever met who knew how to let a body feel.

* * *

I couldn't take it anymore. This isolation. This uncertainty. This constant self-checking about where I can go, how close I can be, where I can stand. Should I wear a mask everywhere? Should I strap a one-metre-long pool noodle to my head when I walk around like they make customers wear in that German café? Who is having the last laugh? I was watching the protests again on the evening news. Those crowds, those skirmishes, the intense close contact. It was everything we weren't supposed to do. It was now doubly wrong. It was the last place we could feel close physical contact. Since there was no way I was taking the LegCo oath with a straight face and since I was the most popular candidate running in my district, I knew I was going to be arrested pretty soon anyway.

I joined the singing in New Town Plaza as an afterthought. As I was strolling through the half-full mall, I spotted Kwok-ying from high school. He was just standing there taking it all in. He hadn't been there so long either. He was trying to understand it, their commitment to a cause in the face of such odds. He had never been very interested in any of it. He only wanted to make money. That's why he joined the government. But he was smart. He would go far if he played his cards right. Kwok-ying wasn't singing, so I joined in. He had been looking at new phones. Then the riot police rushed in and pepper-sprayed a line of yellow-bibbed journalists hovering on the edge of the group. They made them kneel before them in a line, their eyes burning, some of them screaming for water. My blood was up seeing the police wrestle them down, so I probably cursed them all to hell. I rushed over to one of the journalists with my flask of water. Next minute, I was wrestled to the ground. My face was against the cold tile and a knee pushed down on the other side of my head. I screamed as the pressure was intense. His sweaty groin a few inches away from my face. Uniforms can't hide the smell of fear and uncleanliness. The smells you can't capture in the photos.

They've got me down for rioting now. Maximum sentence is ten years. They know me too. I've been on their case for years. They've been looking for something and they won't let me go if they can help it. They'll arrest me and set a court date. They'll take my passport and my travel documents. I have to appear in court again in a month and I'm not hopeful. They have to lay down a marker for the next generation, for the waves of young protesters waiting in the wings, waiting only for the virus lockdown to end.

But I tell myself I've learned so much from the experience. I tell myself that they've made me stronger, these experiences. I'll lose my councillor job and salary, but I must not lose hope. It's when we lose hope that the fighting will end but not the oppression. They'll take more and more because they can. And when the fighting is over, we may truly be the clones John talked about. So, yes, this might all be a fight to cherish the individuality they're asking us to mask. With our masks on, we're less aware of each other's individuality. We become blank faces, ciphers, placeholders for others to fill in with detail. There's a reason so many regimes ask their people to mask up, to wear a veil, to hide their faces. Once we cared why. Now with virus everywhere, our faces don't matter. We're faceless clones. Ten a penny. Pepper spray them all. Water cannon the lot of them. I'll attend my court case unmasked and I'll speak from the witness stand unmasked. I want them to remember what conviction looks like, what this city looks like.

No sooner out of quarantine than I'm back inside a cell. They love their doubling up here. Even the name Pik Uk Prison translates into the Walled-House Prison. Tell me twice in case I forget. John won't understand. He's stuck in his books and movies. But reality is never as smooth as books and movies. I'll invite him to the final court session of the district court. It'll be in English. Give him what he wants. He can write about it then. He needs to feel he's doing his bit with his pen. That's what he wants. To be able to watch us squirm so he can describe it all and feel better about a struggle he knows can never be his.

Oh, but we did squirm! In a sense. I squirmed under him and I'd do it again. He always said our lockdown was our time out of time. Our moment of being sealed off. I was bending over backwards for him. I did it for him. Him embracing me from behind through my clothes in that sweltering lockdown room. Where did that moment come from? From what we've denied ourselves and had denied us and what we know we might never have again. These moments free of surveillance. That closeness and physical contact now denied us from all corners. We'll never open up now. That's what he kept saying to me. But we opened up then. We opened up to each other as we needed to. The hard, concrete floor, those rivulets of scored plaster where the floor tiles had never been lain, eating into my back. But it didn't bother me, lying beneath him. We subjected each other to it, to the physical embrace, but it was ours to give and we gave it willingly.

Phoebe

They come with goggles, umbrellas, water bottles, a water hose to douse burning tear gas, yellow hard hats, plastic binders for steel barriers, and then bricks ripped from the pavements. With each generation of protesters comes an education. You could almost plot the evolution on a graph. If you were into that kind of thing. With each student generation's return to government buildings comes evidence of a little more learned. This time they learned that tear gas could be dealt with. You could see the education blossoming in front of your eyes. Running forward from the front lines the second a tear gas pellet or canister was fired, you discovered you could douse it in water as soon as it landed, its furling spume of smoke giving its location away. Then you smothered it in a towel with your feet and covered the snarling explosion on the concrete in a yellow hard hat. You could buy your group more time in the stand-off with police. What matter that your eyes and throat burned like charcoal, you are being educated in the ways of protest unique to Hong Kong.

As I rounded the walls of the PLA (People's Liberation Army) encampment in Admiralty with legions of young people dressed in black all around me, a high-pitched shout in Cantonese rang out. The words were familiar—Carnie Lim resign—but there was something different about the voice. I looked to my right. A group of young, teenage girls, dressed in black t-shirts, all wearing facemasks, looked red-faced and a little unsure after having shouted out to the group their first rallying cries. There was a slight lull and then applause and then cheering rose up from the throngs around us. They seemed to sense a new voice had been added to their ranks, a new voice that needed support and encouragement. The girls took heart and shouted out more rallying cries and this time the crowd applauded and laughed.

We were the marchers. We were the disenfranchised. The well-educated with no vote and no decent job. The well-educated and underpaid who attended the universities of the third-best university city in the world. If you believe these kinds of tables. If you believe rankings. But, of course, no one believes tables. Only those with a vote believe rankings are real. We marched together, we marched as some of the best-educated protesters in the world. One of the only cities in the world with five universities in the top 100, we marched for our future. We march because we have no vote for our leader and we are underpaid. And then the self-appointed leaders turn around and look surprised. Even Carnie Lim looks surprised on those photos she sits in front of when they interview her. One wonders what a top international education, a top-ranked education, the education of the third-best university city in the world, is for if not to tell you that you should be able to vote for your own leader. That you should aspire to not only get a job but that you should aspire to be able to vote for your leader. Unless you don't believe in rankings. And no one believes in rankings and tables. Unless you don't believe education is what rankings tell you. But who would suggest something of the kind? No one believes in rankings. Everyone believes in education.

We marched as the best-educated in the world who can't buy their own place when we graduate. We marched as the best-educated in the world who can't afford a mortgage when we graduate. We marched as the best-educated in the world who can't move in with our partners when we graduate. The best-educated in the world who will most likely live with our parents until well into our thirties. The best-educated in the world who will see our own language, our very own language, the language we speak to each other each and every day, not some invented language, not some invented character script, pushed out of the school system. We marched as the best-educated in the world who will see well-heeled immigrants from beyond our borders buying up all the new apartments built in our city. The apartments we can't afford. We marched as the best-educated protesters in the world, best-educated by international standards, international standards incorporating basic human rights, rights we have been taught to respect and uphold by the government-funded, third-best university city in the world, the third-best university city in the world that has Carnie Lim sitting at her desk as the chancellor of all of us. The best-educated in the world, possibly only tied with those in Boston and London in the rankings, who are only trying to do what students and scholars do everywhere, to cherish and save our culture in the way our education has taught us we should. These were the young people I marched with. There was no secret ingredient. There was no conspiracy theory. There was no western intruder. Didn't they know that if you make your young people the best-educated in the world, and nurture the third-best university city in the world, there is a chance we might think for ourselves long before we graduate and that we might want to be able to vote for our leader, like other graduates did in every other city that shared the top spot in the best university cities in the world? After all, politics wasn't rocket science they told us.

John

I'm back in the 24-hour McDonald's in Sai Kung on the other side of the peak. The numbers have fallen and there've been no local infections. They still have fewer seats in here than before. At least this one's not in quarantine, but it still reminds me of her.

I hear she's going to court for riot. Another young career ruined. I've seen the careers of the brightest minds of her generation destroyed by the struggle for freedom. Nothing stops them. They put their lives on the line and get thrown in prison for it and denied the chance to travel, the chance to work at what they'd dreamed of.

Those of us not from here never get it. She told me once what it was like. A desperate, all-consuming compulsion becomes a yearning for the high that one experiences in the community, out in the streets. She said, 'Remember that night, that night we spent together in quarantine? well . . . the passion is a lot like that but with the extra feeling of conviction that comes from knowing you're doing it all for thousands of people without a voice.'

I don't try writing about all this any more. Some say writing got us into this mess. Others say, you must be careful what you write these days. Sue called it garbage! The best we can say is, we tried. We educated the young people of Hong Kong in the ways we had grown up with. They looked bored or switched off. We only looked further into where we had come from to find new ways to make them understand, to allow them to find their foothold in this culture we were selling to them. Still, they didn't get it. Still, they responded with caution. So, we invented comparative sessions where we placed our readings of their culture alongside those old readings from ours. We looked for thematic correspondences. We unearthed the theory behind the different offerings, the different comparisons. We laid it all out for them, letting them see how we put it all together. So they could partake. So they could feel part of the process. Still, they didn't bite. So, we made them present on it. We got them to do performances, to act out how they approached this culture, to sing about their trials with it. We let them send us outlines. Any hint of an awakening in this battle with their enquiry into this culture that was not theirs, we cornered and appealed to. Finally, they began to respond. We felt we were getting somewhere. We persisted, devising complex, more delving psychological portraits of the student intent on finding a way into our culture. We wrote up grant applications. We looked for students to sit in control group studies on the problems experienced encountering this culture. We invited international professors over to deliberate on the best ways to open the rich possibilities of our culture to the most uncertain of young minds. We kept it going even when it seemed we weren't getting through. We never gave up. We saw it as our duty. We saw it as the only sacrifice we could make that would be comparable to the sacrifices the young people were making on the streets. Then it hit us one day that we had never bothered to take the time to learn their language properly, to sit with their families for dinner, to listen to their songs, or learn how to cook their dumplings, their soups, their fine jelly desserts. What they had taken into their hearts at our bidding they reflected back to us and it was not to their liking. And the truth is, we did not like it either. For it only showed how to meet them half way. It only showed them a halfway house with no directions back home. But we clammed up. We denied the truth of what we saw. We said they were only throwing it back at us. Throwing it back without taking it into their hearts. It revealed to us in our silent moments, in these moments when there was no need to perform, how, now, the tank was empty. That we had nothing left to teach them. How they had nothing left to learn from us.

Kwok-ying

The government's opening of all karaoke joints, without allowing singing, was the last straw. All the customers phoning in, 'Can I sing?' 'No, you can't sing. But you can buy drinks and even send out for takeaway.' 'Your hot moist breath might go anywhere if you sing.' 'We're sorry, please check back later when we have installed hot breath monitors inside each karaoke mic.'

I've given up getting any pleasure. All my old pleasures are banned. No chance whatsoever of *bok je* for some time. Laura's maybe never coming back. She's stuck in the US. She always hated China anyways. At least that's what she said to get me to move back there with her. She'll never visit here now, not to mention live here.

To be honest I miss my solo excursions to Japan. All those trips I took, visiting all the fancy restaurants. Always ordering sausages. Sausages with mash. Sausages with beetroot. Sausages with cherry tomatoes and salad. Arranging each dish carefully into a cock and balls arrangement and then uploading it to Instagram. Became a running joke with friends. But maybe there was something in it?

Phoebe and John

It's difficult for us to revisit those thirty minutes or so that we spent in the quarantine room together. It's as if we break the spell by trying to describe them. But that's the risk you take when you start a story. When you try to get some kind of truth out.

We called it no-touch sex. Mask up and sanitize he joked. So, we kept our masks on for as long as we could bear it. He even suggested using the compulsory hand sanitizer at the door as baby oil. We could have the least dirty sex ever. He was playful and I played along.

- 'Your nose is showing.'
- 'You know what they say about a nose showing?'
- 'No, what do they say?'
- 'That something else is showing too.'

He bent back the iron rod in the lining at the top of the facemask until it was stuck fast around the crown of his nose.

- 'That's better. Don't want it peeking out too soon.'
- 'I'll get the lubricant.'

He leaned over for the automatic sanitizer dispenser.

- 'Wait a sec. We don't know what it'll do to us. Probably made in China.'

-   'Okay, so we'll just have to take our own precautions. Masks up and no touching.'
-   'I'd say we've got twenty to thirty mins. till we're missed.'
-   'I know. I've never done this before.'
-   'You mean sex?'
-   'No, of course not. This kind of quick in and out.'
-   'Who said it's gonna be a quick in and out?'
-   'Well, you know, it's what one thinks.'
-   'Look, forget the talk.'

He looked like he was about to explode from keeping all his talk in. His throat-clearing he called it.

-   'Me neither, by the way. With a *gweilo* or a geriatric. Take your pick.'

He stripped out of his worn shirt and shorts. His boxers were loose, but at least they were whole. I stripped down to my underwear. We kept the lights off. It was twilight and the fading light played a mix of lights and shadows across our bodies.

Then he glides in in the half-light, moving as close as he could, masked up to the gills. He looked like a cross between a drunk uncle at a wedding and a man playing a spaceship to a child. I was working on myself in the dark, trying to work up to it. I could see he was already up for it. I grabbed it hard as I saw no point in waiting. I didn't want the first load anywhere near me. Probably the result of weeks of quarantine frustration. Every Dai Ma's induced wet dream and more. The second load would be slower, and I knew it would be more for me. It would be for us and for what we were doing here. Our two fingers to their rules.

-   'I don't want what's risen inside you because of others. I want something that I had something to do with. I want the one for me.'

- 'It was always for you. Always for you ever since we met in here.'
- 'Well I'll know when this is gone.'

It didn't take long, that first load. He had been holding back for too long in here, it seems.

Then we started up again.

- 'Masks up. No touching.'

We said it together this time.

He was calmer now. More focused. I was ready too.

He had me moving alongside him almost doubled over to avoid touching. Then we kept gliding in closer and closer like in some weird form on no-touch tango. The music was our breathing, our free-flowing breath. Our bodies were glistening in the half-light with the efforts to glide and not touch with the air conditioner barely working, only blowing hot air. I could see rivulets of sweat running down his back and on to the concrete floor. Still we were barely touching. If we managed to glance off each other, it sent something like a shock wave through us. There was a low moaning coming from him now and I followed too letting out a kind of whining that accompanied my breathing. The moaning came all the stronger from him with the yearning we both felt, but still we held ourselves back, still masked, still not touching. We were conscious of how we still had only broken the one rule. The two-metre rule. It might only be a week of solitary in isolation. It was worth it.

We denied ourselves. Our masks made our visible anonymity charged. The eyes were so intense, I couldn't hold his gaze. And we actually still moaned. Still we glided and groaned around each other and the sweat came running off our bodies. Finally, we had to touch and when we did, it triggered a kind of frenzy. I still can't recall the actions only really the sensations. I knew he held me and that we were on the ground. The tiles had never been lain so the fine ridges of dried tile adhesive dug into my back and then into his. I knew he was then inside and I never thought he would be so I had actually held my breath. Can you believe it? I held my breath for it. It meant I exploded with a kind of howl of release when I felt him inside me. I gave him what he wanted fingering him to bring him on. He was rising higher and his movements were getting laboured and I knew he couldn't do much more and I had his sweat running in my eyes and dropping on to my lips. I was swimming in it and then we glided off each other and I could see he could give no more. I had felt his pulse racing until he was almost gasping for air. We lay panting on our backs on the concrete floor and the semi-darkness seemed to enclose us in its grip. We knew we only had minutes to lie here. We talked.

Phoebe and John

That is only how John might have imagined it before we were even inside the room together. That's what I tell myself. I can hear him denying it now, wherever he is. In actual fact, when we had walked back along my corridor, keeping the required two metres apart, me first with him following, me leaving the door open so he could follow me in, it was all rather different.

We had been starved of touch for so long, it could never have been like what John imagined in the time we had. I had always been slow to commit physically anyway and John too later told me that despite his talk and his play-acting, that his wife, Sue, whom he'd met in Hong Kong, had been his only lover here. He was the kind of guy who'd sit on your bed and lay all this out as if he felt he had to before anything happened. Tedious perhaps and a sure dampener on any spontaneous shows of amorous affection. We were, then, two people who were slow to give our bodies up to the other even if we did share fantasies and desires with each other. Having also been through what the great writer calls a touch famine, we had most likely forgotten how it was done, especially in confined quarters and working against the clock. We had been starved of touch like those once before, in this landmass and in his Ireland, who had been starved of food. My friend, Yangsheng, a teacher from Wuhan, had told me that one of the earliest memories he had was of himself, as a child, lying in the middle of the road with his mouth open. There was nothing at all. The body works in unpredictable ways once offered what it has for so long had to do without. Kafka's story "A Hunger Artist" only tells half the story. We never see him have to give in and take the food. But in the real world, the body will reject food once it has been starved for too long. You try to keep down a piece of dry white toast. You take a bite. Then your stomach turns and the undigested bitten segment comes right back up. We could feel it would be the same with touch and with the countless possibilities that touch opened us up to.

So, when we got into the room, and had closed the door behind us, we knew, in truth, that it had to be for another reason. We wanted to recall the human touch that could only now be felt by breaking the rules. Yes, touch was part of it, and we knew this, but it was also about looking closely, in the flesh, into a full face, and then talking to that face. So, yes, we would embrace each other after we had entered but even this would take a long time. The slow lowering of the face masks (for we had not yet seen each other's faces up close) to reveal the cheeks, the nose, the lips, then the outline of the chin, the way the chin recedes to the neck, the jawline. It was like looking at an outline of a map, enumerating the different headlands that we once had, so long ago that we could barely recall, committed to memory. We took all this in and we smiled. Our smile evoked a shared devotion that echoed the old words this is my body. Oh my! I still can recall the warmth inside on seeing that smile break out. It was a slow but simultaneous and spontaneous eruption of smile. Two smiles may never have been so enriching and so badly needed. It was as if we were smiling not only for ourselves but for a people, striving to remind all of us through our furtive, individual, hidden gestures in this quarantine room, of a shared humanity and fellow feeling that was being outlawed. These were the endangered features of our species. I told myself to breathe it in. And breath, that was the other gift we gave to each other. The simple act of watching another draw breath, a full breath, drawn deep down into the lungs and the bloodstream. It held us transfixed until time again came calling. We inhaled for all humanity. For the gasping millions struggling to retain this elixir from the ether. We inhaled again for the millions masked and the millions infected. We inhaled the air together with a confidence and a physicality we had denied ourselves. We inhaled deeply to remind ourselves that breath was not only a chore or a casualty, a biological feature susceptible to infected micro-droplets, a spirit and bearer of contagion, but the spring and source of life, our preserver so much more than our destroyer. We reminded each other of this.

Then we touched hands, encircling each other's fingers with our own, sensing the charged impulses running through our limbs and our bodies. Like leaves drooping and starved of water, we felt the old life returning as we touched, that openness and responsiveness to the touch of another. It was no longer something to fear. No longer the guilt and regret when a fingernail accidentally brushes an index finger as we receive change or handover money to a 7-Eleven or 24-hour McDonald's cashier. No longer the lingering feeling of being dirty after having felt the brush of another's hand against ours as we exchange groceries, or a mail delivery, or a takeaway, or even after touching a surface that we could just sense had been previously touched by another. We watched our fingers slowly glide in and out of each other's grasp, tracing the line of a finger down to its interdigital fold and a thumb down along its purlicue. Then we joined our palms, pressing the flesh and the cheeks of the palm hard against each other, to feel we were alive, to feel the resistance of another's body. In the end, we had to stand back from each other, extending our arms fully to push with all our might. We broke down in fits of laughter and couldn't sustain it for very long. We let our fingers glide in and out of each other's grasp and then joined our palms again and it felt like some spiritual gesture connecting us to the land and to the spirits of the harvest. It felt like a rite we were practising to rid the land of a plague and the people of the spirits of isolation. We listened and felt the push deep down in our blood and we imagined the blood being charged and enriched by this shared pulse of another.

We listened and looked for the gentle beat of each other's pulse down along the wrist and it came to in our hands in the most attentive, silent listening to the touch of another. For we felt our senses worked together. No longer were they senses strung out and singled out and charged with destruction. No longer were they categorized according to their solitary, specialized features. No, now they worked in tandem, together, in the way all life was meant to work, in harmony, and not broken down into constituent parts that shuddered in shock at this unnatural severance.

And then we moved forward to embrace. We stepped into the presence of the other, into that space we all know where we become aware of the physical closeness of another next to us. Sometimes we speak of how someone invades our space. Well, it was that zone of awareness, that extra-sensory zone of presence about us that we like to call our own. We simply let its awareness and presence envelop us, embrace us, fill us. It was amusing how long it took us to lose that initial fear that we had harboured for so long for the body next to us, for the body by our side. When we had exhausted our exploration of this closeness in the time allowed us, when we could sense the drops of perspiration on each other's neck and forehead from the heat of this closeness and from the humidity of the room with the air conditioning only blowing out gusts of hot air, we began to enjoy how we perspired due to our closeness. We stepped closer and embraced. It was a loving embrace, the kind we would share one time, almost without thinking, with old friends we were reunited with. The kind shared between a father and a son or between a mother and a son, something natural and unthreatening. One of love and fellow-feeling. Neither solely erotic nor frenzied. One that was conscious of the warmth and passion with which we acknowledge our shared humanity and its source in our physicality. We held each other as people no longer did. We held each other as father and son no longer could. As mothers and daughters no longer could. As the aged, the sick and the vulnerable no longer could. We held each other and thought of friends who had lost lovers and friends at this time, of the old gone and buried without ceremony, of those who had been told they were sick by email or by phone call and who yearned for the comfort and the presence of a human face, a warm word, an embrace that was its own healing, its own wellspring, its own source of divinity and sustenance. We held each other and thought of all those we knew and tears came. We watched the tears roll down each other's faces and we were thankful for the time we had been allowed. We watched the tears leave traces of wetness along the flesh and the lips. We touched the tears without wiping them away. We sobbed for what we had denied ourselves or for what had been denied us and we acknowledged now our two bodies pressing close together and heard as one as our arms scrambled to tighten our embrace for fear we might lose contact and then our connection with this emotion. We cried out for the touch and the healing that was being taken from us and that would continue to be taken from us since we knew our cities and towns would never open-up as they once had. We cried for the teenagers growing into this world unable to fully acknowledge what had been left behind. In that moment, we had our own incarnation of sorts, our own transubstantiation when we communed with spirits of the long dead in our own lives, with a spirit of shared humanity of all that was blessed in all of us and that was under threat. For, lodged deep in the life of nature that we fought so hard to protect, was the Life Within. We cried for it for we knew the less we allowed this life, the less we would be able to see it in the cries of the natural world about us.

When the tears had stopped, we needed to rest. Our bodies were drenched from the waves of emotion and the heat in the small room. It was if we were conducting an experiment on the limits of human potential in this small quarantine room. And if we kissed—it's so hard to relive it sometimes—it came slowly and the touch of the lips was like a taste long-forgotten, like the taste of memory itself. We flinch now recalling the sense of it.

We sat together on the thin, narrow mattress. The mattress absorbed our heat and the moisture of our bodies. We knew we had only a short time left before we were missed. We spoke to each other. We talked with each other within earshot, face to face, free of masks.

- 'How are you feeling?'
- 'I'm better now.'
- 'Yes, it seems unreal. I never thought I could share something like this. To feel this way.'
- 'It came slowly but it was worth it.'
- 'Tell me a story. Tell me something about yourself, something you feel you've almost forgotten about yourself.'

I laughed. In that laughter I found something, I found a memory.

Phoebe

There was a girl in Hong Kong who sold feathers. She would dry them in bundles on the balcony of her village apartment. Sometimes feather dust and feather-tips floated down on to the dogs that barked in the lanes between the houses. The mechanical digger that was stalled in the yard in front of the house was sometimes dusted by a fine downy layer of small feather-fingers only to have them blown away in the next breeze from the lowlands. The feathers came in all shapes and sizes. There were long feathers like ostrich tails and there were the short, stumpy feathers that were like squat under-wing feathers, feathers that would only aid the bird slightly in its flights across the Chinese highlands. There were polka-dotted feathers and striped feathers and feathers that looked like they had come from the lush underbelly of the most gloriously white, fleecy, feathered bird. Her grandfather and father had sold feathers before her. When they passed on, they left them behind in many boxes as a memento of their work and their business. Her grandfather had carted the feathers from China to Hong Kong when he fled the political changes. He had set up a shop in Tung Choi Street in Hong Kong right beside Ladies' Market in Mong Kok. At first, he had tried making garments and hats with the feathers, employing local craftsmen cheaply for their hat-making skills and then attaching the feathers. But after a few years he gave up on the hat-making. The craftsmen demanded too much money and he felt they only saw his feathers as insignificant decorative additions like beads or ribbons. He knew the feathers were the most important part. They added life to whatever they adorned. They were the plumages of living beasts of the air and the fields. When the hat moved on someone's head, the feather would still have a special relationship with the air. When the wearer turned her head, she could feel the influence of the feather as it caught the air and worked with or against the wind. Sometimes, this girl would hold one of the almost weightless feathers in her hand and casually move it about to inspect it from different angles. It always amazed her how the light feather commanded the air as it did, tugging gently yet majestically against the rotations she made with it in the air. She imagined hundreds of these feathers on a small living wing, pulsing and moving in unison with the movements of the bird and she understood the force that could lie in these flimsy and light propellers of flight.

Her grandfather and father had passed away now, but their feathers remained. They were stored in a small room in Kwun Tong and she and her mother had not visited it for nearly three years. There were over one hundred boxes of closely-packed feathers. Her mother had put them in storage when her father became ill.

She remembered playing with the feathers when she was a girl. She used to hold them up to her hair and look at herself in the mirror. She would hold a bunch of long peacock and pheasant feathers in a bundle, their stalks knotted in her small hand around a bright sparkling button she had found in the button jar in the kitchen.

- 'Mummy, look at me, look at me.'
- 'You're beautiful darling. You're like a bird. Be careful you don't stick them in your eyes now.'

She never thought such beautiful light things could hurt her, but once, when she took the feathers away from her head, the hard stalk stuck right into her eye. She remembered the pain and how she closed her eye and never wanted to open it again, holding her hands hard against her face to cover the pain. In the hospital, she woke up and there was a patch on her eye. That was why she wore the funny glasses today. One eye was stronger than the other. She was always careful now with the feathers, always holding them away from her eyes, the memory of the hard stalk piercing her soft window on the world making her wince as she thought about how to combine the different colours.

Sometimes her boyfriend would go into her room when she was sleeping or out with friends. When he held one of the feathers up to the light on a bright morning with the sun streaming in from across the Ma On Shan mountain the colours came to life. He could see strands of grey or white glistening in the air that they had once thrived on and glided in. They were like the shiny gills of fish he saw when he walked past them near the pier in Sai Kung. The fish would be flapping on the concrete in the sunshine. The moist gills still had the life of the sea water clinging to them. The life in the fish lent colour to the water that glistened on their gills since the gills were contracting and flexing and casting off the light from the droplets of sea-water in the unique way that only life can add to the moment. Sometimes he thought he could see something of that same life in the feathers he held in his hands in her bedroom even though the birds had been dead for thirty years.

But the more this girl worked with the feathers, the more she started to reflect on their origin. She started to wonder whether the feathers lost something when they were removed from the bird. She began to think they lost the colourful, variegated tones of the individual strands of the feathers that had once tussled with the living currents of air. When she looked closely at the fine strands of the feathers now, she could only think that they resembled horsehair or even, more remotely, human hair. They were stronger, fuller, yet lighter strands of hair that somehow caught the air and fashioned flight from it. She looked closely at the individual strands disturbing the pattern on the feather as she did so. Losing the pattern on the feather and looking at the individual strand, she thought she might learn more about the whole feather and the vast system of flight, but in the end, she realized it told her next to nothing. It was only when she let go her grasp of the individual strand of the feather from between her fingers that she could see how the feather was perfect as a unit. When the pattern again appeared across the face of the feather after the loose individual strands fell back into place, she could make out how the age-old paradox was true. The secret to the feather was not to be found in the individual strands but in the whole that the individual strands created and in the strange and fascinating, airy unity that the strands created as a single feather in a larger batch of feathers on a bird's wing. She recalled too how the word 'weakness' in Chinese was represented with the character 弱 or *ruo* that originated as a pictograph of a fragile plant or possibly even, the scholars say, as a variation of a young bird's wings.

Most of her feathers came from golden pheasants and red pheasants. Her father and mother had worked out a system of naming each batch of feathers before they shipped each order off to the States or to Canada. There were gold and red batches and when she looked at the photographs of the pheasants on the internet, she could see exactly what part of the body the feathers had come from.

- 'I don't like to think about how they got the feathers,' she said to her boyfriend one afternoon while working at her desk.
- 'I bet it was cruel.'

She knew the birds were nothing without their feathers. She tried to imagine the fully plucked birds running around after the plucking, but she knew it wouldn't work. She thought about the plumage and the mating games of the pheasants. The bright colours attracted the right mate. She had started making cocktail hats with feathers as a hobby and soon enough, friends were asking for them. When she thought about the feathers on her cocktail hats, she knew they were doing the same thing thirty years on. She was only giving back to the feathers what they had never had a chance to achieve on the bird. The colours and the long arching stalks were bringing lovers together.

When she sat for hours in her chair, she sometimes remembered the English phrases she had seen in books that used the word feather. She remembered the phrase 'feather in your cap'. She remembered the feather headdresses of the old Indian chiefs she had seen in the old Westerns. Chief Sitting Bull and his gang with all these feathers in their headdresses. The more feathers they had, the more respected they were. She guessed that each feather had a darker story behind it than one about the killing of a pheasant. It made her shudder thinking of all the blood attached to those beautiful headdresses. She imagined the cowboy being shot down by a string of arrows and the Indians riding up to his body. How would they find a suitable feather? Then she remembered that the arrow needed to be guided on its path. There were feathers on the end of each arrow to guide it on its course. She looked up the word for these feathers. Fletchings from the French for arrow *flèche*. They were usually made of goose or turkey feathers. They were sometimes placed at an angle at the end of the arrow shaft so that the arrow rotated in flight for greater accuracy. Feathers didn't only mark the killing, they guided the deadly arrow to its target. She was a little pensive when she picked up her feathers next time. There was blood on these feathers. How could something so beautiful and light be a tool for slaughter? How could the patterns on the feathers be used for anything else but decoration? Feathers, she learnt, like most things, had two sides. The feather was involved at every stage of battle. It was part of the decorative and mating rituals that brought people together, but it was also attached to the arrow as an aid to the kill. And then, at the end, it was used as a decorative element to honour the conquest of a people or an army. She knew she would draw from the positive side of the feather's history. She needed to find the positive in all this. And it was that same spirit that she looked for today when there was so much death and so much destruction.

For her, each feather on a hat marked a new achievement and that was enough for her. Each feather was her own little achievement when she used it as the end-piece on each cocktail hat and brooch. The insertion of the last long feather in a cocktail hat was the sign that the piece was completed. She was awarding it to herself without bloodshed. She was giving something back to the history of feathers by bringing lovers together with her feathers.

And then she remembered too that feathers also helped tell their own story. She thought of the old quills she saw in the hands of writers in the photographs in the books in school. She looked for lines in school related to feathers. Shakespeare was so long, but she would find something. She found the lines from *As You Like It* where Rosalind says that 'a woman's thoughts run before her actions' only for her lover, Orlando, to reply that all thoughts do because 'they are winged'. She liked to think about thoughts being winged. She wondered what he meant. Did he mean that thoughts were all we had that could take flight? That thoughts took us out of ourselves and kept us in contact with the airy world above? She could tell there was more to it, something she was missing. How could her thoughts not be winged and not take flight? She knew that by spending hours at her desk beading felt and feathers together with her calloused hands that she was helping other thoughts take wing for the wearers and their admirers. But once she started to think of every feather as a thought taking wing, she knew she had to move on from feathers. She knew she had to move on to ideas. It was why she had taken to activism and politics. She wanted to really work to make collective ideas take flight.

Sometimes she felt like a trapped bird in Hong Kong. She had dreamed about living in England or France and walking the fields and seeing and touching all those things that the great writers had written about. But she had given that up. This was her place. This was her moment.

That girl was me. This was what I did before the politics. In here in quarantine, in this confined space, I've been thinking about those feathers, about how the feather is a symbol of flight in so many ways, of flights across continents and of flights of the mind. I've been thinking about this and wondering why we are so afraid. So afraid to let our thoughts roam. They can't take that from us. Even masked and imprisoned, with the virus raging, our thoughts can still take shape and take wing.

It hit me again one day, before the virus had arrived, when I went to the bird market in Mong Kok. Throngs of middle-aged men and old men hung around by the entrance with their bird cages. There was such a crowd I could barely pass. Old men with tired, worn faces. Old men pulling hard on cigarettes in the shadows. Old men with old, tough faces, faces that spoke of hard labour, of construction work, even of weariness. Of mah jong parlours and years of the cut and graft of barter and exchange. And here they were with their small birds in their delicate cages. Not a woman in sight. Draw your own conclusions! The place was like a sanctuary to the caged bird. The old men hung out together in the early morning sunshine chatting as their birds sang and their cages hung off railings and off branches and off old nails all around the narrow lanes of the bird market. It was like a scene from an Ang Lee movie. I tried to imagine the men in Song dynasty robes with warriors waltzing across the top-most branches of the trees and the caged birds singing. And that morning, the birds just perched and sang. They were tiny songbirds. Birds that seemed to almost fit the range of their cages. But then I remembered my grandfather and his devotion to his feathers. The years and years spent collecting, treating and packaging the feathers for sale. The belts and boas he would stitch from feathers. His hands working so fast I would think the feathers were part of his hands, that his fingers ended in feathers. But in all that time, I never once saw him with a bird in a cage.

As I passed down the lanes of the market, I could see that some of the men were younger. They wore tracksuits and expensive trainers. They were just a bit older than me. They walked a little nervously with their cages, trying to start up conversations with the older men, with the men who had been coming here for years, with the men who were the champions of the caged birds. I remembered the old passion for the feathers. I remembered how they had made my thoughts take flight. And now here in quarantine, I needed something to take my thoughts off this curtailment, off these cages we have built for ourselves. I must go back to those feathers.

John

I go into the empty campus to teach online. Sometimes at twilight, I'll stand outside a university building built for thousands and there won't be a soul passing. The vast concrete forms are like monuments to a way of life. When I stand back against the railings on the roof of the Fung King Hey Building to get a panoramic view of the campus as it spreads out over the entire hill, the different buildings rise like tombstones in a forgotten sanctuary. The gentle hiss of a building of air conditioners calls to the breeze blowing in off the Tai Po Road and I can almost hear the hollow buildings reverberate with their emptiness. I know that it will be like this for a long time but my learned responses to the environment shape my sense of expectation and it's like I don't want to register the change. I too don't want to force the issue with myself. On this one, I'd rather be a little wistful, a little idealistic.

It comes as a slow-burning sense of loss and then a quiet yearning. The realization that everything has changed. A dull ache inside leading you to almost want to groan aloud. Maybe it is a feeling of heaviness that is not yet dread in the face of a slow realization that learned responses must change, that everything you had learned to base hopes and dreams on had shifted. It only caught you occasionally, maybe if you woke early and the house was still dark. Or maybe when you were leaving the empty office building and you were already at your car and you yearned for the simple distractions that meant you wouldn't be at your car so soon. The glance at the group of students passing, the casual greeting and half-smile from a colleague as you waited for the lift, the words exchanged as you were leaving the building and you held the door for someone whose face you recognized but whose name you couldn't recall.

The classes have been online now for almost one whole term. Students do their best to communicate but they feel more conscious of speaking up if their faces suddenly appear on screen when they speak or even if their names are highlighted. The lag between speech and the moment of response is noticeable and, in noticing that split-second of pause, your courage sometimes leaves you or you reconsider and think your idea might be better left unsaid. Perhaps the greatest lesson students are being fed through all this, to help get them through it the authorities say, is that we're all finding out that we didn't need people as much as we thought we did. I even see it already in the student essays, especially in essays from students who have told me they suffer from depression. Asked to comment on a story from Woolf about how hanging mirrors in your room can lead to misrepresentations and stereotypes, they argue that it's a story about the need to keep your distance from others.

So I decided to write one last piece in the largest lecture theatre we have. Put it to some use. We're paying for its upkeep after all. It's emptiness screams memory, potential and that same sense of expectation. I imagine the voices of a multitude of students rising in chorus. When the vision is over, the vastness of the empty space closes in about me. It resonates at the frequency of my hope and I want to get those vibrations working through my feet, up along my legs, through my loins, into my gut and deep into my heart. For they tell me there is nothing either good or bad, but thinking makes it so. The sun has almost set now behind the hills, but I can still hear through the open doors the whine of a lawnmower and the call of the birds marking the departing light of day.

The whole city was holding its breath before it would be able to pick itself up and go again. Like a prize fighter between rounds, accepting that the odds are stacked against him, acknowledging that he is beginning to see double.

V

Hong Kong
January, 2022

Pangolin

We hear the bats are taking the blame now. We are sorry for them. We have retreated to the deeper woods of Hubei. We have found a new resting place beneath the ground. We have decided to change our identity. Over 400 million years we have seen many changes. This new creature confounds us. Its hunger. Its taste for destruction. We know we are what they call 'marked'. If the Chinese medicine diggers don't get us, the poachers and foragers will. Those of us who remain have retreated to our burrows and our barks. The elders among us are browbeaten. The young cubs call for enforced descaling for all. Desperate times call for desperate measures. They say we must adapt to save our kind. They call for the removal of all our scales using the latest natural techniques and for the transplantation of our long snouts to our foreheads. They tell us they will look like unicorn horns. We need more than masks and disguises. We will also conduct classes, starting immediately, on how to walk on two legs. Without the scales and the snouts and with the horns and the upright walking we expect to be taken for a new kind of mythological beast. They tell us this new creature respects myths. That they look to myth to tell them who they are. We understand this. We will migrate to the southern lands where we are told we will fare better so long as they do not take us for kangaroos. Our long history enables us to imagine ourselves far into the future from where we look back secure in the knowledge that evolution will confirm the wisdom of these changes.

Phoebe

It took time to get over him. I thought quarantine would never end. I found some lines that helped me understand the loss:

> There will be dying, there will be dying,
> but there is no need to go into that . . .

How could I be so cut up about one night in quarantine with all that going on? Sometimes I think I died that night and was born again. There is no other way to explain it. I am thankful that it brought me distraction. Otherwise the loss would have overwhelmed me. The loss of so many. Contact is painful now. It's almost as if I've lost my bearings. Casual encounters seem like pretence; I never know how much to give. And anything that gets serious is too painful.

I never lost my low-level infection. It comes and goes with the weather, never bringing on anything more than a slight cough. Some in the government argued that we should be permanently quarantined out on Lamma, that we should never be allowed to rejoin society. I tried campaigning against it. I did the petitions, organized a march or two but, in the end, my heart wasn't in it. The virus years had infected us in other ways. We grew to see crisis as the norm. Emotionally we were pitched so high for so long, we could never come back down. It was as if I suddenly saw through everything. Everything was superficial. I couldn't attach myself to anything, couldn't apply myself to anything. After two years, I have found a partner. We listen to each other's stories.

Her husband was a victim of the virus. She too needed time with someone who would be there without intruding. Almost like a comforting background noise. That's what we tell ourselves. Anything else is too much. We have time on our hands. We have time to understand why isolation isn't everything. Why everything will be all right if you can only let it be so.

Kwok-ying

It's all a blur now. I don't like talking about it. Truth be told, I can't really talk about it. Since they got rid of Carnie any last pretence is gone. Hundreds of reporters and government officials who spoke out have disappeared. Some good friends among them. They suspended elections after more protests and after the bombs. The virus years brought international recriminations and then the government shipped off faulty medical equipment as well. More lives were lost. This time they had nothing stopping them from sending in the military. Our city is almost gone. I had no choice. What do you do with mouths to feed? Starve or work for the other side? We moved to Guangzhou. No other country was letting us in.

The government produced a report on the virus. It had government approval. No certainty about the origin of the virus. No mention of the pangolin. Its roots traced back decades with a 98 per cent similarity to strains found elsewhere. No one spoke of Wuhan. No one read the report either. It mattered little. The only upshot was that the government expanded. I have found myself questioning sometimes whether there is any difference between viruses and governments.

John

It's been two years since the first outbreak. We live with the after-effects. Price wars and food-rationing brought social unrest. Food shortages in China kickstarted price hikes and inflation soared. Many families couldn't pull through. An already impoverished city was brought to its knees. What little savings we had could only go on food. We were the lucky ones. In the end, when the bombing started and with travel restrictions still worldwide, we decided to stay on.

I never thought I'd look back at the lockdown with a sense of nostalgia. At least then, at the beginning, there was a belief that we were locked in for a reason. It was society responding at a time of need. Community working together. The desperation with which we queued for masks was evidence of an authentic response. It showed that our first reaction would always be to act together to protect others. Then, over time, the lockdown lingered, and it became an opportunity. It had to be explained. There had to be a cause. It was no longer an event an individual could feel she could respond to on her own. Government stepped in to save us from ourselves and to save others from us. There had to be rules and there had to be a lockdown.

And who knows where we are now? When the government trips up and the individual can't be trusted, then the virus leads. It's a lockdown for its own sake.

The period of isolation never really ended. Some people never came out of their houses, their apartments, their rooms. The epidemic gave way to an intense epidemic of loneliness. But it was a loneliness people came to tolerate. Even in classes where people show up for face-to-face teaching, there is caution in the air. People are suspicious of any contact. They sit a couple of seats apart. Some of my students spent the majority of their teenage years in isolation, home schooling or learning online. All the students in my classes still wear facemasks during lectures. All of them wipe the desks down with alcohol wipes. We had a small cluster of infections towards the end that went viral and we're still dealing with the impact. The vaccines available were never fully trusted. International student numbers fell dramatically and it hit the rankings. International staff stayed away. The budget from the government was cut. A new social isolation app took off too. The developers called it OVID. It was basically an app that plotted transformations in cell structure and told you the location of anyone nearby who had been infected or in contact with someone who had been infected. Sometimes you'd see groups of people on their phones move *en masse* across a train carriage away from some unsuspecting bystander. Would it be easier if they made us all wear yellow badges?

Older people retreated into themselves. Most of them still felt afraid and they couldn't shake it. They only went out very early in the morning to the local greengrocer or the empty church. The majority of older people in big cities never left their homes again. In the small towns of Italy and Spain community life has almost disappeared altogether. Family life has never been the same.

And what of the epicentre? What of Wuhan? Well its eleven million people had to soldier on. On social media, animosity towards Chinese medicinal practices continued and eventually the government in Hong Kong had to close all the Chinese medicine shops. There were protests on the streets but in the interests of business and tourism they eventually had to give way. No one travels to Wuhan. It became a city apart. Even if a flight transfers there, people avoid it. In many ways, it became an inhabited Chernobyl. Mao would have been distraught to see the city in which he spent so many of his summers reduced to a stagnant, shunned city. I still recall my tour of the city a few years ago. They had just built an enormous new history museum. The prize exhibits were the centuries-old imperial bells that were rung at the Beijing Olympics opening ceremony and the tomb of the old Marquis Yee of Zheng complete with its eighteen separate chambers for the eighteen concubines who were buried with him. I remember looking down into the separate compartments thinking how far we had come. How could we ever have been so barbaric? Some of the compartments for the concubines were so small they could only have been inhabited by young girls. The reality of this barbaric practice from thousands of years ago jarred with the slick glass and steel complex. I left the city feeling Wuhan had the perfect mix of cultural treasures, modern urban shops and parks. I told myself I would return again to give it more time.

Phoebe

I look back now and see the lockdown as the calm before the storm. When the broader security measures were signed in, the protests erupted again. They sent thousands of troops in. Everything was banned, so everything went underground. We were all in and out of prison.

During the lockdown, they had called it the 'open-up'. It was going to be like V-E Day. There would be tables all down the streets. House parties and parades. The day we would celebrate the end of lockdowns. But the open-up never came. There was no clear endpoint. No line in the sand between lockdown and open-up. No foreign enemy had finally been crushed as in Berlin in the '40s.

I looked at the old photos of the crowds celebrating for V-E Day. The singalong down the streets of London. Arms locked, marching as one, soldiers and sailors alongside their partners. Eyes closed as they march in song. Churchill waving down at the sea of people in Trafalgar Square.

They kept putting off the date. We were never ready, never safe. There was too much of a spike. The second, third, fourth wave is coming. We can't open-up too soon. It was like a state of limbo. At least we could all avoid hell. But we began to forget what we missed. The cold comforts of isolation and no thrills mornings and evenings locked us in hard and fast like no government decree ever could.

Then they said there would be a date for the open-up. We could see it. We rehearsed it many times in our heads. When open-up came, we would move out on to the balconies and into the parks. At first, we would move in regimental celebration, but in the end, with the crowds milling about, many still masked, we would eventually give way and hug someone in a spontaneous rush. But the memory of their touch hounded us all the way back and it was only when we'd scrubbed ourselves clean for twenty minutes, changed all our clothes, turned off the lights and waited till the sounds on the streets died to silence that we really felt home.

Sue

Sometimes through the long hours looking after Sam, I think about love. I ask myself what it is all about. I think about love through the objects I spend my time with every day. John does so much, but the mother is so often the go-to person, what the child knows and smells and needs, from the labour, to the birthing, to the nursing and early feeding and then the expectations of others and the way they look at you here. When I wake to his cries, his endless cries, when John has taken the sleep out of him, I try to see the love in everything I do, in everything I see around me. I try to see this world in terms of the love I need and in terms of the love that is still healing inside me. A husband's love is like an old sock fallen down behind the headboard gathering dust, but a new son's love is like a flower blossoming. A husband's love is like an old curtain riddled with damp and dust brushing against an old grate, but a new son's love sparkles like dew. A husband's love is like an old blanket lodged in between the mattress and the wall, gathering bits of old insect, but a son's love pipes up like birdsong. A husband's love is like an old apartment wall with the paint peeling around the window frames, but a son's love colours the morning with rainbows even from the deepest of sleeps. A husband's love is like an old toy discarded in the corner of the room, but a son's love wrestles you awake to a mother's love that is the root of all. A son's love is a cry to a father's love that is like a JCB raising you, upsy-daisy. A son's love stops its crying lifted high by a father's love, but a mother's love lets the crying be until sleep comes like the giving of life. A father's love is like a bottle, fed-upon and drained and then cast aside so the formula spoils.

John

In the end we never left lockdown. The life we created out of nothing through lockdown became the life we had to take hold of to live through the political lockdown that came after. We thought seriously about leaving but then the restrictions on Sue's visa made us reconsider. Then there were all the attacks on Chinese people worldwide. We hunkered down for the long haul. Our balcony became a world apart.

I even found myself reassessing lockdown. After feeling a sense of impending doom for so long in our lives even before the virus came along, lockdown gave us focus. We started to believe that if we acted a certain way, things could get better. We hadn't felt this with such conviction for a long time. We had an end point in mind. Everything would open up after a few months if we could only hold the line. There were road maps and staggered government plans for how we would open up. We could dream about the coffee we could have in our favourite café at the end of August. To believe the opposite, to believe either that things would never open up or, worse still, that the freedoms we still had under lockdown would also be targeted when it ended was kind of unthinkable.

What I learnt from lockdown was to change my expectations. I had to make this new life as meaningful as it could be. How I understood a window of opportunity or a sense of possibility had all drawn from what I had long taken for granted. Intoxicating as these ideas were, I had to check myself every time they came calling. Initially it felt like ridding yourself of an addiction, but an addiction that both your body and mind told you was *really* good for you.

Our balcony became a world apart. I had eggplants, tomatoes and chillies growing in pots all across it. Sue bought a bread machine and sourced flour from whenever she could. With the bombs and the police response of firing indiscriminately, we needed somewhere to focus on the little bit of growth and creation left us. I heard one day that Phoebe had lost an eye to a rubber bullet. I hoped it was not her good eye.

I used to take Sam out on the balcony. He had no interest in the tomatoes. He only wanted to pull them off the plant. But sometimes, as I raised him high and he looked out over the squat village houses, out to the sea where the pearl divers once swam, I could almost forget that the city was under siege. He would stare out for a moment, still before language had come, and then with a few frustrated stretches and without even a glance at the new eggplants, I knew he already wanted to go back inside.

Last Mid-Autumn Festival, we climbed the steps to the roof of our building. Sue told me the story of the ancient princess, Chang-E, who stole the potion of immortality from her lover, Hou Yi, only to be banished to the moon. A golden moon shone large just above our horizon and Sam was calling out 'Moon, Moon'. We needed these beacons of love even more at times of separation, when you were separated from those you loved. In the golden light of the moon, I thought of those I will never see again.

And how did I get back here after the lockdown? Sue let me return to the flat after three months of living in a small place in Fanling. She said she wanted Sam to have his dad around. I have still not told her everything. I needed to write it out first. To see if this would help me explain it. I know I will tell her soon. For the first two months after I was back, I was self-isolating in my own room. There were still occasional outbreaks, but this time I wasn't self-isolating because of the virus. In the end, living together without touching or even talking felt worse than quarantine. We embraced one morning as we watched Sam munching on a piece of bread running off smiling into the corner of his dungeon. The days of listening to their Cantonese from my small room, only understanding the odd phrase, made me realize how much I was missing. Sue's friend, who was a mid-wife, used to call over too. I used to listen to their words, words I now felt twice removed from. My wife and her mid-wife friend speaking Cantonese, speaking about birthing and its physical recuperation. I sat alone in a damp room full of books, reading when I could. The words of the women in the next room hummed with the kitchen extractor fan and their meaning went right through me. I was only able to pick up the greetings, the basic formalities, some of the adjectives. Most of the content eluded me. I'd be sent out to get plastic bags for the bin for nappies from the local hardware store. Hadn't they always told us we were different, men and women? I can't remember never feeling it; the yearning to see a girl with a paisley blouse; the fear with which I walked into a room of women right into my twenties; the kind of talk I had with my mother versus the kind of talk I had with my father.

A few weeks after I got back, my sick boy was sitting in a hospital incubator struggling for breath. But in a calm moment, I'm sure we saw him dreaming. His limbs were flailing at images and sounds we couldn't fashion. He took his mother's milk in a bottle for feeding in the nursing room. I was asked by the nurses to wait outside. It was all men wandering the corridors, nursing phone screens. Passing ships without ballast or direction.

The cries of my son all evening until he sleeps are like the soundtrack to my slow recognition inside over months and years. That there is something called individuality and that it emerges from the closeness my son still feels and senses and remembers as his by birth and through birth and because of birth, a closeness that must slowly recede over time. That feeling of closeness, the closeness recalled from once being part of another's body, part of his mother's body, is given up over time. It's no longer there with each breath or each heartbeat. It's no longer there with each move and grab and twist that arose out of the blood of another and was only made possible in the body of another. I knew that in order to learn to cherish a world without the old closeness we had taken for granted, I would have to get even closer to Sam and to Sue. To watch how they grew together in the memory of that closeness they once shared.

As I am walking with him, holding my sick fourteen-kilogram bundle, I hear him doing that thing with his vocal chords where each breath lets out a kind of meditative moan. It's like he is humming himself to sleep. A hum on every breath. When Sue and I hear it, we know he is close to sleep. It's a kind of self-lulling I need to try myself. I focus more on what I'm doing. I look to the future and what he might remember. I look to the past and imagine my own father doing this with me. The nights and nights of walking and lulling that never get remembered by the child. Those moments when you tell yourself you are putting things off. When you silence the questions about what you are gaining from all this. The virus years made me forget these questions and they made me give myself up to the daily cares that saved me. From somewhere inside I started to listen to a new kind of understanding. A voice telling me—you are learning how to care for another. I didn't want to listen. I had to learn that care wasn't about self-denial or self-sacrifice. The care of others close to you is its own reward. I believe it now. The virus years brought it all home. The work I did for so long, sometimes out of habit, was no longer the most important work. The virus years taught me this. Without the virus, I know I would have continued chasing ghosts. The virus turned everything on its head, and I realized there were things I had been doing for years that were not important. Lying on the floor in the empty house in Cork, riven with anguish and guilt, I realized care too had a calling and it asked us to make a choice. Even the immortal Chang-E had to make a choice to love forever from a distance. At times of social distancing, whatever opportunity I had for care through touch and contact was precious. Back with Sue and Sam I lapped up the only tenderness and contact the virus allowed me. I would learn from that celebration of touch I had shared with Phoebe. It was already helping me reimagine my time with Sue. After months in quarantine and isolation, to get it back was a gift. There was no way I was giving it up again.

Sometimes I think it's harder for a father to believe he's a father than it is for a mother to believe she's a mother. So, when I take Sam up, his arms flailing, his small mouth gaping, the tongue curved like a bell for maximum vibrato, I look for the father in me. I cup him in my arms, nestling him into my breathing chest, his head rising on my breaths like waves beating against a shoreline as he starts curling for sleep. I told myself he was fathering out (finding out about his father), rooting himself into the body that could never be the mother's, but that still reeked of something familiar he sensed he should know. He was asking me to discover how to be a father through him. 'Fathering Out' I called it. As he chafed against my skin like a memory that will stick, I knew he was fathering out my feelings all the better to rise me.

Phoebe

John sent me this whole thing in a big, padded envelope. It arrived at the old district office. He wrote that he wanted me to have it as a gift. Some kind of memento for the time we shared. Will these guys ever learn? No one cares. Part of me wanted to bin it there and then. How can we still push the old mantra about getting it down, remembering, when so much has changed? When so many of the memories cause so much pain? I don't know any more if it does more harm than good. But I knew I couldn't bin it. No one has ever written me so much. I can't read for very long. The weak eye tires easily. I like to read those pages about quarantine sometimes. I dip in, remember, and it helps me feel the person I was. I momentarily forget the chaos around me. I know he's only trying to explain it to himself as well. Even the possibility of one other person reading something you wrote, gives you some perspective. So I read it sometimes when I need to forget, so I can go again. When there is time to forget, time for recharging, for remembering why we struggle, why we need to fight on.

Princess Selina

In the 24-hour McDonald's the seats are all full again. Don't they know who I am? I will have to move to the benches outside. I won't sit on a bench outside. Princess Selina doesn't sit outside an establishment. Today I know what I'm wearing. Everything has a story. I have the two wide-brimmed, straw hats, the three facemasks, my favourite Italian high heels, the long navy trouser pants I got through Harrods, the ones with a lace trimming at the hem that almost drags along the floor. The attendant is looking at me. She's more attractive than the usual *Dai Mas* they have serving. She looks positively polished. This recession must be dragging us all down.

- 'I am Princess Selina. I am a millionaire's heiress. A Millionaire's Heiress.'

Why does she stare? Is something not right with her? I'll rest my large gold holdall here on the counter beside their little keypad. I'll put my plastic, see-through box, the Japanese Home Centre one, right beside it. Important people bring their possessions with them. Like the British. My father couldn't bring his wealth with him. He left it to me.

- 'Just let me get out my purse and Octopus card. They're in this plastic box somewhere. I'll have the muffin with the pork and cheese. And a cup of your finest coffee.'

I'll just rest my box here. The papers of my life. My inheritance papers are in here. And the deeds to the apartment. I never leave home without them now. The proof that I am a millionaire's heiress. It's taking a great deal of time. Don't they know who I am? Better remind them:

- 'I am Princess Selina. I am a millionaire's heiress. A Millionaire's Heiress.'

Ah, there's my order. There really are no seats. I'll lean on my plastic box on the counter and stare them out. I'll stare at all of them long and hard, sitting on their small islands of tables and squat stools. All these unwashed early morning risers, munching in their tracksuits and hiking gear. The stinking old men, savouring their hotcakes. The only hot meal of the day for them. Maybe I'll just leave. In no mood this morning for causing a fuss. They'll be surprised to see me go. Even the mighty can sometimes swallow their pride. Princess Selina will leave the premises.

The bag of takeaway fits nicely in my plastic box. Don't look back now. Acknowledge that nice lady at reception. She was a pleasure to deal with. The Sai Kung plaza is rather empty. I'll just make my way over to Starbucks. I have photos of myself to caption for my scrapbook. For the letters I send out to penfriends. I can put my screen up in there for a bit of privacy. Powder my nose. Lipstick my lips. My God it is wet today. The hem of my trouser legs is soaking. Princess Selina never stops to fix a hem in public. Those Filipina ladies will be out shopping soon. Their shopping carts are so ugly. And the old village ladies will be getting their veg. But I've beaten them to it.

This plaza with its tall, Chinese parasol trees is so empty. No one can see me this morning. All the work I put in. I have walked past Starbucks. My mind was elsewhere. On Papa perhaps. Never mind. It's too late now. I'll take this nice alley between Government Buildings and the vegetable shop on the corner. Feeling a little weary anyway. Best to go back now. Make a pot of tea. All that work dolling up for nothing. Our kingdom. My father's kingdom. Handed down to me. His only child. These steps are a struggle today. I'll take the elevator. It makes me sick, but I'll hold my breath. Those stinking smokers. There we are now. Home sweet home. My papa's kingdom. Passed down to his only daughter. His princess. Princess Selina. And didn't I earn it? All those years caring for him. I gave up my whole life to it. Saved myself for him. I could have been a lady. With a proper gentleman. But I gave it all up for him. Captain Fung. Merchant Sea Captain of three commercial vessels. No one enters my apartment, my kingdom, but Princess Selina. I haven't let anyone in since Papa passed away. He lost the vessels and the going concerns during SARS when I looked after him on my own, giving up my best years. How he was wined and dined by the British Navy. That night in the Peninsula with Admiral Parker. Me on Papa's knee. Catching the eye of all the men in shirts and ties. Mind you, he never told me until the very end. How much he'd lost. The shock was too much. At least I have this apartment if not the land it is built on. The land is only ours for so long as they will let us keep the land. Its in our Basic Law. Those barbarians. But I am Princess Selina. I don't worry about that now. Princess Selina. That wonderful evening in the Peninsula and Admiral Parker's embrace.

She closes the door behind her and takes out her best china. Papa left it to me. Why not? Why not use the last of it? What am I saving it for? That walk this morning has really taken it out of me. I must loosen the trouser pants. Yes, that's it. The Fortnum and Mason Tea. British tea. British hospitality. Princess Selina will never be caught out. Never embarrassed. And no one has ever been inside here. Now, where did I put the cups? There are so many bags in here now. I can't find anything. And it's getting a little dusty. English Breakfast Tea. His favourite. Heavy on the milk. Scald the pot! How he used to shout it. Let it draw! I'll sit back in my chair. I'll just sit back for a moment and wait for the tea

to draw. I am Princess Selina. I've been waiting such a long time.
A whole lifetime. Pour the English Breakfast Tea, will you? And
take off that hat in the house! He was always so angry. Even before
she has taken her first mouthful, the aroma floods her nostrils.
'Papa. Papa. You're being naughty. Take your tea now. Let's use
our English. There's no one here now. Let's use our English as we
look out on those ships leaving the pier for the last time.'